soul of eli

Pamela Gail

Contains situations not intended for children 16+

Edited By Brittany Montano Management, LLC
and Michele Edits

Published By Brackish Publishing
brackishpublishing.com
Copyright © 2025 by Pamela Gail

This book is dedicated to the men in my life. My husband, Rick, and my sons, Anders and Grady. Without the three of you, I would have never been able to push through all the self-doubt and create something I'm proud to publish.

prologue

SIX YEARS AGO

This is the day Izzy and I have been waiting for since Christmas. It's been two long months, and I dread looking out the window. What if it's raining? What if we have a weird cold snap? What if our parents change their minds at the last minute?

I could barely sleep last night from worrying so much about everything that could happen to keep us from building the treehouse. Our dads promised to build us a treehouse in the giant sand oak that sits between our houses over a year ago. We've been asking them to get started every week. Now, our dream is finally coming true.

Quickly rolling out of bed, my feet hit the floor, and I race to my window to pull up the blinds. The sun isn't out yet, but it's not raining. Yes! I press my palm to the glass, warm. Perfect! The only thing stopping us now is our parents. Well, my mom. She's the one who keeps finding reasons to put off building the treehouse. Now, all I can do is hope she didn't change her mind or convince my dad to change his.

My dad said if Izzy and I help, the treehouse will be mostly ready by the end of the weekend. That's all the incentive I need. I'll do anything to get this thing built so we can have a clubhouse all to ourselves. It's gonna be epic!

Even though I didn't sleep much last night, I woke up extra early. Izzy said she'll be ready early, too. Izzy is my best friend and lives right next door. We've been best friends since she moved here when we were four. We like a lot of the same stuff—playing soccer, reading fantasy books, and watching scary movies. We both love old horror movies. Halloween is my favorite, but Izzy's is Nightmare on Elm Street.

Izzy doesn't have any brothers or sisters, but she always wanted one. She tells me I'm lucky to have two older sisters, but she's wrong about that. They aren't any fun and don't like hanging out with me. Izzy is the only cool girl I know. Most of them do boring stuff like play with dolls and wear makeup.

My sisters are a lot older than me and are constantly talking about boys and going on dates. Molly is seventeen and I saw her kissing her boyfriend yesterday. Yuck! It was totally gross. Emma is sixteen and calls me a bratty, little kid. What does she know? Teenagers are so stupid. I hope I'm not mean like them when I get older.

It's seven on the dot when I pull on a pair of jeans and a t-shirt. I've been awake for almost an hour already this morning, but my mom told me not to come out of my room before seven. The wait was pure torture, but there was no way I was going to disobey her. I've been extra good all week.

Quietly, I open my door listening for any sounds of life. The smell of bacon and waffles fills the air, and I can hear my parents talking downstairs. I rush down the steps, taking them two at a time and jumping from the fourth step.

"Eli," my dad warns as soon as my feet thud against the floor.

My parents are always telling me to be careful, so I don't get hurt. They worry too much. Boys are supposed to do dangerous things and get hurt once in a while. Last year, I broke my arm twice, but not from jumping down the stairs. I wrecked my bike jumping off the ramp my dad built and over some old trashcans. It would've been super cool if I'd made it over the last can, but my back tire clipped it and sent me sailing through the air. I landed on my left arm and broke it in three places. I had to have surgery and then wear a cast for three months because it took longer to heal than expected. My mom made Dad get rid of the ramp.

The second time was only two weeks after I got my cast off. I fell from the top of the monkey bars at school and broke my left wrist. It wasn't so bad, and I was only in a cast for six weeks.

We aren't allowed to sit on top of the bars, but none of the teachers were paying attention, and some mean girl threw another kid's sweatshirt up there. So, I climbed up to get it for him but slipped and fell. My teacher yelled at me when I came back to school a couple of days later. She didn't even let me explain why I was up there. Since that day, my mom gets upset if I do anything even a little dangerous. She's always been overprotective. She's the reason it took my dad a year to buy the materials, and another two months after that to get started on the treehouse. She's worried I'll fall out and get hurt badly.

"Sorry," I mumble, walking into the kitchen. "Are you making waffles?"

"Yes. And bacon and grits. You guys need a hearty breakfast if you're going to be working outside all day." Mom smiles and pretends to be excited, but I heard them talking a couple of days ago. She kept saying the treehouse wasn't safe. I guess my dad won since we're building it. Anyway, it will be safe. Dad and Mr. Chandler would never let us build something without taking all the best safety measures.

"Yummy! Is it ready?" I ask as my stomach growls.

This is my favorite breakfast. I love waffles, bacon, and grits. Eggs are super gross, but I have to eat them a few times a week when my mom cooks them. She has a rule about us eating what she cooks and not complaining about it. I'm not a picky eater. I like almost everything she cooks, so I don't understand why she forces me to eat eggs. I'm glad she didn't make any today.

"Almost. Grab three plates and some utensils and set the table," she instructs.

"Sure," I happily agree.

I quickly set the table. Not only have I been extra good lately, but I've also been helping with more chores.

My sisters never get up before noon on the weekends. I usually sleep later than seven, but not as late as those two. My bedtime is earlier than their curfew, even on the weekends, because my parents still treat me like a little kid even though I'm ten. I'll be eleven in five and half months. My birthday is always the same week that school starts back. It's a stinky way to celebrate your birthday. Izzy's birthday is a month before mine, so we always celebrate together. Our parents throw us a big end-of-summer birthday party about two weeks before school starts with bouncy houses and waterslides. There's no fence separating our houses, so the party takes up both backyards, and we invite everyone we know. It's a blast! This year's going to be even better since the treehouse will be ready. It will make the perfect fort for a Nerf war, too.

Mom puts a spoonful of grits on my plate, and I help myself to the waffles and bacon on the table.

"That's enough," my mom scolds as I drown my waffles in syrup. She takes the bottle from me and sets it out of my reach like I'm some baby. The syrup is the best part of waffles, but I never get to have as much as I want.

I need to eat fast so we can get started. Dad piles his plate with food while Mom pours him some more coffee. I took a sip of my mom's coffee once when Molly dared me. It tasted like burnt tires. It was disgusting. How can adults drink it every day?

As soon as I'm done eating, I place my plate in the sink.

"Come on, Dad. Let's go! Did you call Mr. Chandler and tell him we're almost ready?" I ask my dad.

"Let me finish eating, then I'll call him."

"Ugh! Hurry up," I beg.

"Don't rush your father," Mom scolds. "Go brush your teeth, sweetie." I rush upstairs. "Get a jacket. It's chilly this morning," she calls as I reach the top step.

My bedroom window faces the backyard and I can see Izzy sitting on the pile of wood our dads bought last night, bouncing a soccer ball from one knee to the other. Yes, she's ready! I brush my teeth as fast as possible and grab my black jacket before rushing back down the stairs.

"Izzy's outside," I yell, racing through the kitchen and out the back door, careful not to slam it.

"Hey!" She waves.

I toss my jacket on the ground. "Hey!"

"Are you ready?" she asks.

"Yeah, but my dad's still eating breakfast."

"Mine is getting dressed. Why are dads so slow?"

"I don't know."

"Wanna kick the soccer ball while we wait?" she asks me.

"Sure." I shrug.

I haven't been into soccer this year as much as I was in the past. Soccer's okay, but I started playing baseball two years ago, and I've gotten pretty good. I like it more than soccer but kicking the ball with Izzy is always fun. She's tough and really good. We played on the same team until we were nine, and they started separating the girls and boys. It's kind of stupid if you ask me. Izzy's a better player than most of the boys on my team. I guess it doesn't matter anyway since this is probably going to be my last year playing soccer. I haven't told my parents yet, but I think they'll understand. When I get to middle school, I have to choose between baseball and soccer because the seasons overlap, so in fifth grade, I want to spend my extra time getting better at baseball. It's tough to make the middle school team. I need the extra practice if I'm going to have a shot.

Izzy's ten like me, but she's already in fifth grade. My parents held me back when I was little, so I didn't start kindergarten until I was six. Izzy got asked to play on a twelve-and-under traveling soccer team this year. She's the youngest player on the team, and the only one who's ten. She said there are two girls who are eleven, and everyone else is twelve. It's a really big deal. Anyway, she doesn't get all whiney and cry if she doesn't win like the girls in my class. She also beats me most of the time. My mom says I'm too competitive and should let her win even more because she's a girl. That's stupid. No one should get to win just because they're a girl. Plus, Izzy would smack me if I let her win, and that girl can hit hard.

"Are you excited about the treehouse?" she asks as the ball sails past me. It was an easy pass, and I should have been paying attention.

"Well, duh. I've been waiting for this for practically my whole life!"

"Your whole life? Really?"

She laughs with a roll of her eyes. "Well, the past year seems like forever."

"It's gonna be epic!" she exclaims.

"Yeah. We can go up there every day and hang out," I agree.

"It will be like a clubhouse just for us. No parents."

"And no sisters!" I shout. Izzy laughs at my outburst.

We've been kicking the ball for close to an hour when our dads finally make it outside. It takes forever for them to set up the worktable and tools before we can get started.

"Marcus, do you want to cut wood and hand it to me?" Mr. Chandler asks my dad.

"Sounds good, Bob."

Dad measures and cuts pieces of wood, then hands them to Izzy and me so we can pass them to Mr. Chandler, who's on the ladder. He builds houses for a living, so he knows exactly what to do. My dad knows how to build a few things and fix stuff around the house, but he's a boater. Our family owns the marina, the bait and tackle shop, and a charter fishing company. We live less than a mile from the Gulf of Mexico, and our house sits on the waterway on the northeast side of the island where it curves before joining the river that runs between Ashton Bay and the mainland.

Dad takes people out on fishing trips and even sells some of the fish and shrimp he catches to local restaurants. The marina is a cool place to hang out. Izzy and I walk down there every morning after breakfast in the summer. We swim in the Gulf, catch crabs at low tide, and drink sodas out of glass bottles from this ancient vending machine.

"Eli," Mr. Chandler calls.

"Yeah?"

"Climb up that other ladder and come hold this board for me."

I look at my dad to make sure it's okay. He nods his approval, so I scurry up the ladder. If Mom sees me, she's going to go nuts.

"Hold it right there as tight as you can," Mr. Chandler instructs, pointing to where he wants me to put my hands.

"Okay," I respond nervously, trying to keep my balance on the ladder and hold the wood.

"Got it?" he asks.

"Got it," I confirm.

I use all my strength to hold the board while Izzy's dad uses the nail gun to connect two pieces of wood.

"You can let go." I start to climb down the ladder, but Mr. Chandler stops me. "Wait one second. I need help with these boards, too."

I help him with four other boards. When we're done, I carefully climb back down the ladder. After cutting a few more boards, my dad moves the ladder to the other side of Mr. Chandler.

"Okay, Izzy. Your turn."

"Really, Mr. Sterling?" Izzy asks excitedly.

"Yep! Climb up and help your dad."

She does the same thing I did — holding pieces of wood while Mr. Chandler attaches them. It's so cool that our dads are letting us help with the fun parts. I thought they were just going to have us pass wood and tools to them all day.

By the time we stop for lunch, the floor and two walls are finished. That leaves two walls, the roof, the ladder, and the ramp for after lunch. Last weekend, our moms went to the junkyard and found some old crates and one of those giant, wooden spool things. They cleaned the crates and added cushions to make chairs, then refinished and stained the spool for a table. It's going to look awesome when it's finished.

"I made some sandwiches," Izzy's mom calls from their back porch. "Wash up and come eat."

"Race ya," Izzy yells, taking off toward her house.

"Hey!" I yell, running after her and catching up just as we reach her porch.

"Beat'cha!" she gloats.

"Yeah, well, you cheated."

"You're just mad 'cuz I'm faster."

We laugh as we push each other, trying to be first inside. I win, reaching the bathroom two steps before Izzy. We wash our hands as we laugh and splash each other with water.

"I hope you two aren't making a mess," Mrs. Chandler calls from the kitchen, which makes us laugh even harder. "Just clean it up."

Mrs. Chandler is always cool about us making

messes as long as we clean up. My mom would be mad if we splashed water all over the bathroom. She likes everything clean all the time. Izzy's house is way more fun than mine. It's not dirty, but it isn't spotless like ours. My mom hates clutter, and everything has a place. She gets mad if we don't put our stuff away. I'm the only kid I know whose room is always picked up.

All the adults are in the kitchen when we get there. The counter is full of platters with ham sandwiches, chips, and fruit. I take a sandwich and some chips then turn toward the table.

"Get some fruit," my mom insists.

I put two strawberries and one apple slice on my plate. Fruit is delicious, but I don't want to waste time eating it today.

We eat our lunch as quickly as possible and beg our dads to hurry up about a dozen times before they stop talking to our moms. Grownups take forever to do everything. It's so frustrating.

"Ready to get back to work?" my dad finally asks.

"Yes!" Izzy and I shout together.

"Throw your trash away and put your dishes in the sink," Mom insists.

Izzy gathers our trash, and I pick up our dirty plates.

"Thanks for lunch, Momma," Izzy says, tossing the trash in the can.

"Thank you," I tell Mrs. Chandler, placing our dishes in the sink

Mrs. Chandler kisses Izzy on the cheek. "You're welcome, kids."

"Lunch was great, Mary. Thank you," Dad adds.

"I'm going to the grocery store," my mom tells us before kissing my dad.

"I need a few things. Why don't I ride with you, Evie?" Mrs. Chandler offers.

"Sounds great. Maybe we can pick up some burgers and have dinner on the dock tonight," Mom replies.

Yes! Dinner on the dock is my favorite. Our families get together a couple of times a month and eat on our dock, then we go swimming.

"Be safe," Mom reminds us.

My dad watches as Mom and Mrs. Chandler climb into the car. Mom slowly backs out of the driveway. As soon as her car is out of sight, my dad looks at me.

"Do you want to learn how to use the circular saw?" he asks me.

"What? Me? Uh, yeah!"

I can't believe he's going to teach me how to operate the circular saw. My mom would freak out. That's why he was watching her leave. I thought he was being old and gross.

"Listen very carefully. First, we need to measure the wood. Look at the plans and find the third wall."

I look over the plans for a minute. "Here." I point to the wall on the plans.

"Good. What is the measurement for the top beam?" he asks.

"Six feet."

"So, these wooden beams are eight feet. Grab the

tape measure and measure six feet, then mark it with the pencil. Then, measure it again just to be sure."

I carefully do as I'm told. When I'm done, my dad checks the measurement.

"Good job, son. Help me lift this onto the table."

Once the piece of wood is in place, my dad continues with his instructions.

"Put on these safety glasses. Always make sure your hands stay clear of the blade. Hold the wood here with your left hand and pick up the saw with your right. Line the blade up with your pencil mark," he instructs, and I do exactly what he says. "Good. Listen carefully before you do anything else. You're going to pull the trigger to start the saw then push the blade against the wood, holding the saw and wood steady until it cuts all the way through. Got it?"

"Yes."

"If you get scared or confused, just let go of the trigger, and the saw will shut off."

"Okay," I say hesitantly. I'm excited but super nervous.

"Go ahead."

I pull the trigger and slowly push the saw until it passes through the wood, and two pieces lay before me. I let go of the trigger, and my dad takes the saw from me.

He beams at me with pride. "Great job, son," he praises.

"Thanks." I smile.

It feels good to please my dad and do a good job. I like learning new things.

I help him cut the rest of the wood while Izzy helps her dad nail some pieces together. Much too soon, my mom pulls into the driveway, and my job cutting wood comes to an end.

It's getting late in the afternoon when the last wall is finished, then we nail the pegs in place to create a ladder.

"Everything's ready for the grill when you guys are done," Mrs. Chandler tells our dads when we're working on the last two pegs.

"Why don't I start the grill while you help the kids finish up?" Mr. Chandler suggests.

"You got it," Dad replies.

"Wait! What about the roof and ramp?" I ask.

"We'll get that done tomorrow," Dad promises. "Then Bob and I will help carry the seats and tables into the treehouse so you and Izzy can situate everything right where you want it. How does that sound?"

"Okay, I guess." I'm a little disappointed that we can't finish today, but it is starting to get dark, and I'm hungry. "Can we eat in the treehouse tonight?" I ask. "We don't need a roof or table for that."

"Yeah, can we?" Izzy echoes.

"If your mothers agree," Dad tells us.

We both race home to ask our moms. Mrs. Chandler will say yes in a heartbeat, but my mom will need some convincing.

"Please, Mom," I beg. "We'll be careful and clean up all of the dishes and trash, and we won't spill any food," I promise.

"Eli, we're eating on the dock with the Chandlers. It will be a nice family dinner."

"But Molly has a date, and Emma went to her friend's house," I argue. Is it a family dinner if my sisters are gone? "You and Dad and the Chandlers can have an adult dinner," I suggest.

Before my mom can answer, her phone rings. She holds up a finger telling me to be quiet while she takes the call. I pace the kitchen listening to her half of the conversation with Izzy's mom.

"That was Mary," she says as she ends the call. "She thinks it will be fun for the adults to have a double date while you kids eat in the treehouse. I guess that will be fine."

"Really? Thanks, Mom!" Way to go, Mrs. Chandler.

I said the same thing, but I know Mom was about to say no. Izzy's mom probably knew that and called to save the night.

A few minutes later, Izzy and I are in the treehouse with our dinner. Izzy's mom made homemade sweet potato fries with her special seasoning blend, and my mom made a chocolate pie while our dads grilled hamburgers and hot dogs. Mom even let me have a soda with dinner. She *never* lets me have soda, that's why I have to sneak them at the marina. It's the perfect end to the best day ever.

Izzy's face lights up after we finish our meals. It's the same look she always gets when she has exciting news to share, or one of her great ideas.

"What?" I ask.

"Two things. First—I drew some pictures to hang in here," Izzy says, placing four drawings on the floor. "Which ones do you think we should use?" Izzy loves to draw and paint. She's a great artist.

I look through the pictures thinking about each one. "I like these two for the treehouse." One is a sunset over the water, and one is a treehouse that looks almost like ours. She drew it last year when we first started talking about building it. "Can I have this one to hang in my bedroom?" I ask, holding up the one of the marina.

"Sure. I agree on these for the treehouse. I'll save the one of the boat to hang somewhere else.

We hang the two drawings with the tacks she brought out.

"Come here!" Izzy motions for me to follow her down the ladder. She walks to the other side of the tree and points to a hole just above her head.

"Second—look at this cool hidey-hole!" she exclaims. She stands on her tippy toes and reaches in. "This old coffee can fits perfectly. "Open it," she instructs, handing the can to me. Inside, I find a letter written in her handwriting.

Dear Eli,

I'm super happy that we built this treehouse together.

We are going to have so many fun adventures in it.

You're the best friend ever!
Izzy 🩶

"Won't it be fun to leave each other notes when we're too busy to hang out?" she asks.

"Yeah! Great idea," I agree.

The older we get, the less time we have together. Her travel soccer team takes up a lot of time, and if I'm going to play baseball in middle school, it will take a bunch of my time, too. The note thing is a great idea.

Looking up at the treehouse, it hits me that this is a big deal. We built something together that we can share as friends for the rest of our lives—just Izzy and me.

chapter
one
PRESENT DAY

T he treehouse sits low in the oak tree on the property line between Izzy's house and mine. Our dads helped us build it when we were kids, long hours spent over a weekend then several Sunday afternoons to put on the finishing touches. It was worth it. Six years have passed, and it's still one of my favorite spots. A few boards need to be replaced, slowly rotting from the salt air, and it could use a new coat of paint inside, but it's held up well.

I climb the pegged ladder and make my way inside. At six feet tall, I can no longer stand up straight in here, but that doesn't matter. This is where I belong, where I escape from life. Most of my time is spent at school, playing baseball, or working at the marina. That doesn't leave much time for friends, or really any kind of a social life, but there is one person I will always make time for — Izzy. She's my best friend and still the coolest girl I know.

My shift starts in less than an hour, and that's only

because it's Monday. My dad doesn't make me come in before school on Mondays since it's the only day I don't have practice after school. Instead, as Dad puts it, I get the privilege of going to work at five in the afternoon to help close the store and clean up from the day's fishing excursions. Most days, I have to come in before school and make sure the boats are gassed up and clean for any fishing expeditions, and that the store is stocked and ready to open. I hate getting up at four-thirty, but if I'm not at the marina by five, I don't have time to get everything done before school. I rarely get to bed before midnight. With practice going until seven or later most days, then dinner and home-work, weekdays are long. The weekend isn't much better. If I'm not at a game or practice, I'm at the marina. The money's good, but the hours suck. I want to have time to be a teenager, partying with my friends and dating.

Today, I rushed home after school, so I'd have a few minutes with Izzy before work. I miss hanging out with her. About the time I settle on the floor with my back against the south wall, she pops her head in the doorway as if appearing out of nowhere. I laugh at her antics. Izzy can always make me laugh no matter my mood.

Her long, blonde hair is pulled back into a ponytail the way she usually wears it. She's wearing jeans and a band t-shirt, her personal uniform. Izzy loves music. She has more band shirts than any guy I know. Today, it's Johnny Cash. Izzy's an old soul. She doesn't follow much new music, preferring older bands like The

Beatles, The Rolling Stones, Led Zeppelin, The Doors, and Fleetwood Mac. She has great taste in music and has taught me a lot about it over the years. Music isn't really my thing, and I rarely listen to it if I'm not with Izzy.

"Hey," she greets me, plopping down on the floor across from me and stretching her legs out. Her legs barely reach halfway across the room while mine almost touch the opposite wall. "How was school?"

"It was school." I shrug.

"I know. 'I go to school so I can play ball,'" Izzy mocks. "School isn't that bad. You need an education."

"I'm smart enough. I can do without two and half more years. At least I won't have to deal with college."

Izzy is homeschooled and doesn't understand the daily drama and extreme boredom high school days entail.

"There's no guarantee you'll make it to the majors," she reminds me. Izzy does her best to keep me grounded. Sometimes, it actually works.

"True, but there's a decent chance. And there's always the minors. Anyway, if baseball doesn't work out, I'll be slingin' fish at the marina."

"You hate that job. You don't want to take over the family business, and you know it."

She's right. I work there because it's my dad's company. When I turned thirteen, he didn't give me a choice. He started me out with a few hours each weekend, but he's slowly added hours and responsibilities over the years. At least having my dad as my boss, I can work the hours that benefit my practice and game schedule, but I despise the job. That's not entirely true. I like fishing and working the charters with Captain Mike.

I hate working with my dad. He's unnecessarily hard on me because I'm his son. I don't want to be a fisherman for the rest of my life. I prefer fishing for fun, but I don't know how to tell my dad. He's going to be disappointed. He knows how important baseball is to me but acts like the majors aren't a career choice or real option. He ignores my dream and constantly talks about me taking over the family business. It's not like my sisters are going to work there, so I guess he's holding out hope for me.

Molly is twenty-three. Last year, she graduated from college with a teaching degree and took a job teaching first grade. She's getting married this summer to the guy she's been dating since she was fifteen. Jack is nice enough. He's a country club kid with a huge trust fund. Molly is set for life. Must be nice.

Emma is twenty-two and will be graduating in May with a marketing degree. According to my mom, she's brilliant when it comes to designing ad campaigns. My dad is having her do a whole new marketing plan for the marina. It's a waste of money, if you ask me. But, whatever. It's not my money. She's been dating Jared for two years and expects a ring soon. Why are my sisters in such a hurry to get married and settle down? I want to play major league baseball, date a bunch of girls, and *never* get married.

Izzy doesn't agree with most of my recent choices. She calls me out when I need it even though I don't listen. She thinks I'm headed down a dark path. We've had a few arguments about some of my decisions these past few months, but, ultimately, she is my biggest supporter and cheerleader.

"You're right. If baseball doesn't work out, I don't know what I'll do."

It's the only thing I love, and it's all I choose to understand. I'm smart, but school has never been my thing. For the past several years, my main focus has been baseball. All my extra effort is put toward improving my game. As a result, school and work have suffered.

"Well, there's always the marina," she teases.

"Shut up," I laugh. Glancing at my phone, I realize I've sat here longer than intended. "I wish I could stay. If I leave now, I'll only be five minutes late for work."

"Then go," she commands, gesturing to the ladder. "You don't need any grief from your dad."

What would I do without this girl?

chapter
two

"You're late," my dad barks as soon as I step onto the dock. He must have been in his office and seen me walking down the boardwalk. Why else would he be waiting on the dock?

He's on my ass constantly about something. If it's not the crappy job I'm doing at the marina, it's my grades or the way I play ball. He's worse than the coaches.

"Five minutes. Get over it." Before I can walk away, Dad steps in my path. I know better than to talk to him that way.

"Son, you need to get your priorities straight," he snaps, a mix of anger and disappointment in his eyes. "Where were you?"

"At home. I lost track of time. Sorry," I bark.

"You were in that damn treehouse again, weren't you? That shit's for kids. It's time you grow up. I'm tempted to tear it down."

"What? Why the fuck would you do that?" If he tears down the treehouse, I'll do something we'll both regret.

"Watch your language. The treehouse is coming down if you don't start showing a little maturity. I'm tired of you being late. It happens too often."

"Then fire me!" I yell, walking off before he has a chance to respond.

He's being ridiculous. The treehouse is Izzy's and mine. He has no right to tear it down. I barely spend any time there anymore. He makes sure most of my waking hours are filled with work and baseball. I'm sick of it all.

When I reach the trawler, Captain Mike has just finished deboarding his passengers. I like working with him. He treats me as an equal, not like a little kid. Truthfully, I don't mind working with any of the boat captains except Captain Marley. She's kind of a bitch and acts like she knows more than anyone else. She definitely knows her way around a boat and these waters, but she's rude and condescending. None of our regular groups will go on excursions with her. My dad needs to fire her, but for some reason, he keeps her on year after year, complaint after complaint.

This afternoon, I'll help Captain Mike with the day's catch and then clean the boat. Even though we live in North Florida, the nights get cool in February. It's miserable when I get wet washing the boats, which is practically impossible not to do, so I keep extra clothes in Dad's office.

The Gulf Coast in Florida is a great place to grow up—white-sand beaches and warm weather most of the year. While much of Florida's Gulf Coast has clear, blue-green water, Ashton Bay's water is murky and brackish. The area is littered with great fishing spots, and it's easy to catch a variety of fish year-round. The shallows are the perfect place to dig for oysters and clams. Sometimes I eat them raw right there on the shore.

Fishing and hanging out with Izzy and my other friends are my favorite things to do in my free time. Ashton Bay is a small town near the bend of the panhandle. There's always something to do here—fishing, sailing, swimming, kayaking, the farmer's market, restaurants, shops, and museums. During the spring and summer, we have a huge influx of tourists.

Our house isn't far from my dad's company, Sterling, Inc., which includes Ashton Marina, Bait Your Hook, and Gulf Charters. Ashton Marina has a few permanent residents who live on their boats year-round, but most slips are rented anywhere from a few days or weeks, sometimes a month or more. We get boats from all over the world with people looking for an escape. It's the perfect place to dock your boat then a drive, or flight, to nearby destinations is quick and easy. Bait Your Hook supplies fisherman, guests, and residents with everything from bait and fishing gear to groceries and clothes. Gulf Charters takes individuals and groups for deep sea fishing adventures in the Gulf of Mexico.

My dad has built a thriving business and made a ton of money. I understand why he wants me to take over the business, but I'm not passionate about it like him. One day when I'm too old to play ball, it might be something I consider. Truthfully, I like being on the water and fishing as long as I don't have to deal with my dad. It's been a long time since we saw eye to eye on anything. He's a good father, but he doesn't understand me and never knows when to back off.

He's the one who pushed me to get involved in sports when I was a kid. He had me playing t-ball and soccer when I was three. Then he added basketball, football, and lacrosse as I got older. I hated the last three and only played them for one a season each. Soccer was fun when Izzy and I were on the same team, but it quickly became boring when they separated us. When I realized that I was good at baseball, I dropped soccer and never looked back. I love the game, and now, I'm glad my dad pushed me, but sometimes he makes it difficult. Having him constantly pressuring me to practice and be the best almost forced me to quit a few times.

In two and a half years, I'll graduate and can move out. Once I'm in the majors and out of his house, I won't have to deal with him berating me and breathing down my neck.

"Eli, my man! What's up?" Captain Mike greets me.

"Not much. Catch anything?" I ask.

"Hell, yeah. Good fishing day. They went to grab

some coolers from their trucks." He nods his chin toward the guys who passed me on the dock. "Can you get ice?"

"On it."

For the next hour, I pack four coolers of fish, icing them down. They had an awesome haul of flounder, black drum, and sheepshead. Damn, I need to go fishing soon. Sheepshead is my favorite fish, and this is the best time of year to catch them. They're in abundance during the winter months when the water is a little colder. They feed on shellfish, so they have a sweet flavor. It's been too long since I've fished for fun. I take charters out when we're busy and my dad needs the extra help, but I lack the time to do anything for fun.

Once the coolers are packed, we load them into two trucks. As the group drives away, Captain Mike turns to me.

"I'm glad you're here. Grab a cooler from the shed and meet me back at the boat."

"Don't you have one on the boat?"

"Yeah, but we'll need another one." He jogs off before I have a chance to ask any more questions.

Shrugging, I walk in the opposite direction and find a medium-sized cooler in the shed before making my way down the dock. My dad is standing in the doorway of the bait and tackle shop eyeing me. What is he doing? He doesn't need to check up on me. I do my job when I'm here.

Shaking thoughts of my dad away, I climb onto the boat and set the cooler next to the built-in coolers where each day's catch is kept cold until returning to shore. Captain Mike is there with a large barrel of ice. He opens the hatch, where he keeps everything he catches, revealing a bunch of fish. I whistle at the impressive sight.

"Put some ice in the bottom of the cooler you grabbed," he instructs.

I do as I'm told while he does the same to his personal cooler. He tosses a few flounder in each one. Next, he pulls out a sheepshead and hands it to me.

"There are six more. Put this one in my cooler and the other six in yours." Under the sheepshead are two black drums and another flounder. Mike takes the flounder and one black drum and tells me to put the other in the cooler I'm packing. Then we cover all the fish with more ice. Mike had a huge haul. Today, the number of fish caught on Miss Maggie is one for the books. It's been a couple of years since I've seen that many fish in one take.

Mike's boat is named after his wife, who died when they had only been married two years. He raised their only daughter, who was one at the time, by himself and never remarried. His daughter is in her late twenties now and has two sons. Mike lives next door to them and brings his grandsons to the marina all the time. He's a good man who loves his family.

"Let's get these coolers loaded," Mike says.

I help him get both coolers onto the dock and wheel them up the ramp to his truck. After loading his cooler, he turns to me.

"Did you walk over?"

"Seriously, Captain Mike. Do you think my parents are going to let me drive anywhere I can walk?"

"Alright, I gotcha. In that case, we'll put this cooler in the truck, too. At the end of the night, I'll drop you and the fish at home."

"Wait, what?" I'm confused.

"That cooler is for you and your family. I know how much you love sheepshead."

"But I put six of them in that cooler. That's too many," I argue.

"Take them home and enjoy. You haven't been fishing in weeks, and I know your dad doesn't bring much home. I want to share the good day I had with you," he says, clapping my shoulder.

"Wow, thanks!"

"Let's get everything cleaned up so I can get you home. We both have fish to clean."

He's right. It will take me a couple of hours to clean and prep all that fish, but it will be worth the time to have a freezer full of sheepshead. My mood brightens at the thought and the rest of the night passes quickly.

By the time we finish washing the boat, it's after eight. Dad has closed the shop, and his office light is off. He makes every effort to be home by seven to have dinner with the family. Of course, lately, that's him and Mom since my sisters have moved out, and I'm not usually home by then. My mom is a stickler for time, and we eat dinner at seven on the dot every night. She leaves me a plate warming in the oven so I can eat when I get home, but sometimes I miss having a meal with my family. Growing up, we always ate breakfast and dinner together. It's weird eating alone most of the time now.

"That about does it," Captain Mike exclaims, locking the door to the boat's cabin. "When does the season start?" he asks as we walk up the ramp.

"Practice started a couple of weeks ago. Our first game is next Friday, so we have just over a week."

"Nice. You pitchin' the first game?"

"Yeah."

"Home or Away?"

"Home. We're playing Hampton Beach. I hear they're pretty good this year," I tell him.

"No one can beat y'all. State champs four years running, and now they have you pitchin'!"

"I hope you're right. It'd be cool to go to State again."

Not many freshmen get to start at the varsity level, but the team's best pitcher graduated, and the coach saw me play in middle school. Last year, he took a risk and started me instead of the junior. It pissed a lot of people off. We won every game I pitched in our first seven games and lost every game Sam pitched. After that, no one said anything to Coach when he started me. Now, I'm the number one pitcher on the team, and he only plays the others when my arm needs a rest. Coach told me last week he's going to play Mitch more this year so he's ready to back me up after Sam graduates. Mitch is a decent pitcher. Coach is making the right decision.

"What time is the game on Friday?"

"Five."

Captain Mike pulls out his phone and taps it a couple of times. Then he types something.

"Okay, I'll be there. I don't have any trips scheduled for that day, so I marked off for the afternoon."

"Thanks, but you don't have to come to the game."

"Are we gonna have the same argument again this year? It's gettin' old. Text me your schedule so I can get the home games on my calendar."

He has come to almost every home game since I started middle school. Mike is a huge baseball fan, and it's nice that he comes to watch me play.

"I will. Thanks, Captain Mike."

I hop out of the truck and pull the cooler to the edge. Before I can lift it off the tailgate, Captain Mike is at my side.

"Let me help. That cooler is heavy, and your dad and coaches will kill me if you get injured on my watch."

I don't argue. Coach would have my head if he knew what I was really doing at the marina during the season. He lectures me all the time about protecting my arm. As far as he knows, I do laundry and stock a few shelves. He wouldn't be happy knowing I work the charters. Chances of getting injured are greater on the charters than at the bait shop.

Mike watches as I wheel the cooler to the back of the house where my dad has a covered concrete slab containing a large table with a few drawers, a sink, and a deep freezer. Everything needed to gut, clean, and prep the fish for the freezer is here. There's no way my mom would let us bring smelly fish into the house before it's been properly cleaned, deboned, and packed.

"Thanks, Mike," I call. He waves as he retreats to his truck.

chapter
three

My alarm blares promptly at four-thirty the next morning. I smack the snooze button and turn over, pulling my pillow over my head. The alarm on my phone never wakes me, so I started using an old clock that can wake the dead. It's obnoxiously loud but does the trick. The alarm sounds a second time. My body screams at me to shut the thing off and get some more sleep. It took me until after ten to get all the fish in the freezer and clean the prep area. Leaving fish remnants out overnight would entice every wild animal for miles.

By the time I inhaled the food my mom left for me and did my homework, it was after one. I'm not at all prepared for the history test I have this afternoon. If I fail, it will pull my average dangerously close to a D. Athletes aren't allowed to play if any class drops below a C average. Right now, science and PE are the only classes that I don't have Cs in. I can't afford to be benched. Scouts won't start actively looking at me this year, but I need to keep my stats up. If I'm sitting on the bench, my stats will suffer, and no one will give me a look next year.

The alarm sounds a third time. If I don't get up and get to work, Dad will never let me hear the end of it. I don't see his ass getting up in the middle of the night. Nope. He has someone else open the shop at six-thirty while he strolls in around nine every morning. Sometimes on the weekends, he doesn't go in at all.

Slowly, I crawl out of bed and pull on jeans and a sweatshirt. Jogging to the marina instead of taking Dad's truck gives me an extra workout. The cool morning air stings my face, and I'm grateful for the sweatshirt.

The first items on my list are gassing up the boats that are going out today and making sure they all have the right number of life jackets, fishing rods, extra hooks, lines, sinkers, and gloves. Then I ice down water in a cooler for each boat and stock the galley with snacks. I make sure the basket of basic supplies is refilled with sunscreen, ponchos, lip balm, seasick meds, and hand sanitizer. Moving into the head, I refill the soap dispenser, make sure there's plenty of toilet paper, switch out yesterday's towels with clean ones, and restock the first aid kits. When all of that is finished, I take the dirty towels and toss them in three washing machines located in the shed behind the bait shop. By the time the boat captains arrive, the towels will be ready for the dryer. One of them always tosses them in the dryer, then my dad folds them and puts them away when he comes in. Getting five boats ready takes me over two hours.

It's already well after seven as I jog back home to shower and get dressed for school. I grab a PopTart and eat it right out of the package while I walk the mile to school. Homeroom starts at eight-fifteen, and I'm opening the front door to the building as the second bell rings. I know it's the second bell because the halls are empty. Late. *Great.* Coach will be on my ass at practice. It sucks having him as my homeroom teacher. Every time I'm late, he makes me run laps after practice.

"Thanks for joining us, Sterling," Coach barks as I try to sneak into the room.

"No problem," I snap back.

It was stupid, but I don't need to start my day with him on my case. I shouldn't have hit the snooze button twice.

"Wanna try that again?"

"Sorry, Coach," I mumble.

"We'll deal with this at practice. Find your desk," which is his way of saying I'll be running even more laps since I talked back to him. Great way to start the day, Eli.

The day continued to go downhill. My lunch account was overdrawn because I forgot to ask my mom to add more money *and* I left my wallet at home, so I didn't have any cash or my debit card. The history test was worse than I expected. I couldn't focus, and I only answered about half the questions. By the time practice started, I was starving and in a shitty mood. I played like crap, and Coach rode my ass about it the whole practice.

It's after seven, and the field has cleared—except for Coach and me. His favorite punishment is making us run laps. And I don't mean a few, I mean upwards of five or ten miles. Tonight, he thought my attitude and lateness deserved ten miles. It's bullshit if you ask me, but I can't afford the repercussions if I express my disdain to Coach. I'm on lap twenty-five out of forty. My legs are on fire, and my side is killing me. Pushing through, I pass Coach watching me from the dugout, adding another lap to my count. It'll be a miracle if I make it to forty.

Another five laps, and I've slowed to a jog. My stomach turns, stopping me in my tracks. I lean over and dry heave a few times. If I had eaten lunch, it would be all over the track right now.

"Nine more," Coach calls through the bullhorn. *Asshole*. Can't he see me struggling? "Let's go, Sterling."

I slowly start jogging again. It takes longer than it should for me to finish the last nine laps, and walking the last two was the only reason I didn't end up face down on the track.

I'm breathing heavily as I make my way past Coach to the locker room. I grab my bags, skipping the shower, and head out the door as Coach reaches the building. He blocks my way.

"What was that shit on the final laps? When I tell

you to run, I mean *run*." I knew walking would piss him off, but I don't give a shit. "Don't be late tomorrow and come with a better attitude," he scolds. "You might be a great player, but that doesn't give you the right to treat your teammates like shit or stroll into school whenever the mood strikes you."

"Yes, Coach," I reply angrily.

I don't have the strength or mental capacity to have a conversation. It wouldn't do any good. Coach sees what he wants to see. I push my way past him. My legs are burning and cramping, but the rest of the team left almost two hours ago, so I can't bum a ride with anyone. I have no choice but to walk home.

Before going inside to shower and eat, I climb up to the treehouse. I need to talk to Izzy. She's usually up here waiting for me to get home from practice. As soon as my eyes land on her sitting in the corner opposite the doorway, I relax. She has her back to me, leaning over our spool-shaped table, likely drawing.

Tonight, her hair is pulled up on top of her head in a messy bun, and she's in jeans and a red Ashton High Anglers baseball jersey. When she isn't wearing a band shirt, she's wearing one of our team shirts or an Ashton Bay Marina shirt. That basically describes her entire wardrobe.

"Hey! How was practice?" she asks without looking at me.

"Sucked. I played like crap, and Coach made me run laps."

"I'm sorry you had a bad practice. I drew a picture of you on the field."

I lean over to see the picture. I'm on the mound in my uniform, getting ready to throw a pitch. It's a younger version of me, possibly from middle school. I look like a kid, probably thirteen or so. It's amazing what a few years and puberty can do. Now I'm taller than everyone else in my family. Contrary to that picture, when I look in the mirror, a man stares back at me. Damn, she's talented.

"Impressive," I praise.

"Thanks." She blushes. Izzy has no idea how talented she is. "What's bothering you?"

"Nothing," I lie.

"Something." She takes my hand and pulls me down next to her. "Tell me."

She looks at me with those caring, blue eyes that can see right into my soul. She knows me better than anyone else.

"I need help with history. I failed my test today."

"Oh, I'm not any good at history."

"You're good at everything."

"Can't your teacher help?" she offers, ignoring my compliment.

"I don't have time to stay for his tutoring sessions. They're on Tuesdays and Thursdays. I'm either at practice or a game."

"Won't the coach understand if you're late to practice because you're at tutoring?"

"No. He expects us to be at practice on time every day. No excuses. No exceptions."

"Even if it means being benched for your grades?" Izzy questions.

"I don't know," I say, shrugging.

"Talk to him," she encourages.

"I'll think about it."

"Good. Now, go get a shower and some rest. You smell and look like shit."

chapter
four

Once I'm back inside, I quickly shower before rushing downstairs for some food. The PopTart I ate for breakfast is long gone. I shouldn't have practiced without eating. It isn't safe or healthy. I'm a little surprised I didn't pass out while running those laps.

"Slow down, Eli. You're going to break something," my mom calls as I jump over the last five steps and land with a powerful thud that shakes the glass figurines on the hallway shelves. She hates it when I run in the house or jump down the steps. She should be used to it. I've been doing it for as long as I can remember. Actually, I was doing it before I can remember. I have a scar over my right eye where I fell and hit the wall, busting my head open and needing eight stitches. I was only two and jumped down the last three steps. It was too many for a little guy. Guess I should have started with one, not three, but I was a baby and didn't know any better. If that trauma didn't stop me, nothing will.

"Sorry," I mumble. "I'm starving. What did you and Dad have for dinner?"

She smiles at me. "Sheepshead. There's a plate in the oven for you."

"Thanks, Mom! You're the best." I open the oven, revealing a plate with two large pieces of baked fish, corn, asparagus, and a sweet potato. "This looks great."

"There are rolls in the breadbasket and salad in the fridge if you want any," she offers.

"Sounds good."

After leaving my plate on the table and grabbing a few rolls, I put some salad in a bowl and cover it with blue cheese dressing. Mom likes to cook big meals at night and save the leftovers for lunch. Tomorrow, she'll pack me a salad with pieces of fish on it to take for lunch. She doesn't pack me a lunch every day, but I know I won't have to eat cafeteria food the next day when we have this much food at night.

I'm surprised my mom is still downstairs. It's after ten, and she usually goes upstairs with a glass of wine to take a bath and read around nine. Every once in a while, she'll stay up later to see me.

She pours herself a glass of white wine and joins me at the table.

"How was your day?" she asks. It's hard to tell if she's interested in my day or knows something already.

"Pretty good," I lie

"How does the team look this year?" Dad asks, coming in from the living room and sitting next to Mom.

"Good. We've got some talent." I stifle a groan as I take bite of the fish. So good.

"That's great. Think you'll make it to State?"

"There's a decent chance."

"Did you have a good day at school?" Mom asks.

I shrug. "It was alright, I guess."

"I'm glad you're home," Mom says, patting my hand. She's always been overprotective, but it's gotten worse since I started driving. Even on nights when I don't have the car, she worries.

I'm shoveling food in as fast as I can when my dad clears his throat. They share a strange look and focus on me. Okay, this is weird. They don't make a habit of hanging out while I eat. Something is definitely wrong. Now, I'm rethinking their line of questioning.

"Son, we need to talk to you," Dad starts. "Your coach called tonight." Yep. They were baiting me to see if I'd squeal on myself–like that's ever going to happen.

Great. "Why?" I play dumb even though I have a good idea of what they talked about.

"Where do I start?" Dad asks in exasperation, throwing his hands in the air. Oh, this isn't going to be good. "You were late for school, which seems to be a problem recently. Then you had the nerve to talk back to Coach in front of the class and again at practice. He also got an email from your history teacher, who said you failed your test today. It seems you didn't really try since you only answered part of the questions. Look, son—I don't know what's going on with you lately, but you need to pull your head out of your ass and get your priorities straight. We've had this conversation too many times lately. You pull the same crap at work. Half the time you're late. And the other half— your work ethic stinks. You're sixteen and about to be a grown man. You have responsibilities that come before anything else. Baseball, work, and school should be the only things you're focusing on. Not friends. Not girls. Not video games. And *certainly* not that stupid treehouse."

"The treehouse isn't stupid!" I yell. *Excellent comeback. Out of the things he listed, that's what you focus on. Good job, Eli. That's going to make him support keeping the treehouse.*

"Don't raise your voice at me," Dad barks in return.

Ignoring him, I continue. "I don't date. I rarely spend time with my friends outside of school and practice. I don't play video games. I have one console that hasn't been turned on in *five years*. All I do is work, go to school, and play baseball. I do have my priorities straight, but it's all too damn much!"

"Clearly, you aren't making the effort that school, baseball, and work deserve. I don't know what you're doing to waste so much time, but if you don't start putting in the time to study, you're going to start the season on the bench."

"I'd have more time to study if I wasn't working twenty or more hours a week."

"When I was your age, I worked more than twenty hours a week and kept my grades up. You are *lazy*. Stop making excuses and start putting forth some effort," my dad says, his words cutting me.

"I'll see what I can do," I snap, tossing my fork on my half-empty plate and storming out of the room. I'm still hungry, but that conversation caused me to lose my appetite. Taking the steps two at a time, I run up to my room and slam the door. I'm doing the best I can. Why can't my parents see that? I'm busting my ass every day, but I can't get ahead. My friends all have time to party and date while I work my ass off.

Collapsing onto the bed, my mind is all over the place. My parents are disappointed in me. Coach is pissed. Chances are high that I'll be benched for the first game. My grades are in the toilet. Everything sucks right now. I want it all to stop. I can't keep this up much longer.

"Eli," my mom calls after I ignore the knocking.

When I don't respond, she opens the door. Quickly, I wipe my face on the pillow, but I don't turn to face her. She doesn't need to know I've been crying. Mom sits on the edge of my bed and rubs her hand down my back. It's the same comforting gesture she's used since I was a kid. It's her way of telling me she's there when I'm ready to talk. It's nice, but I don't believe she really means it anymore. Tonight, my dad led the conversation, but there have been plenty of similar ones between Mom and me the past few months. She usually doesn't hold back. Evelyn Sterling is a strong, opinionated woman. She will cast judgment on you in a heartbeat. She won't talk behind your back because she doesn't believe in gossip. She says it right to your face.

She doesn't wait for me to speak. "He means well. Your dad is worried about you. We both are."

"Don't defend him!" I bark. I wish she'd go away and leave me alone.

"We love you, Eli. We want the best for you."

"But neither of you will listen when I try to tell you what's best for me."

"We're your parents and have raised two other children. We've learned a thing or two in our lifetime and know what's best for our children."

"No, you don't."

Why won't they listen to me? Why can't they see I'm drowning? For almost a year, I've been barely hanging on. I feel like everything is caving in on me, like I'm losing the battle of life and the weight of it all is suffocating me.

They don't understand. My parents are brushers. They brush anything bad aside and pretend like it didn't happen. Then they smile and move on as if everything is perfect. Well, it's not. Nothing is perfect. Nothing is even good right now.

"Eli, listen to me."

"No. You never listen to me, and neither does Dad. Get out. I have homework to do."

Sitting up and pushing past her, I climb out of bed and open my backpack. She can sit there all night for all I care, but if she isn't going to leave so I can sleep, I'll pretend to do homework. Mom waits about ten minutes before she gets frustrated, sighs heavily, and starts to leave my room. She pauses at the door.

"Good night, sweetheart. I love you."

I don't respond as she closes the door behind her.

Most days, I don't see much of her. Either I'm rushing out in the mornings, or she's in bed when I get home. Sometimes I miss the talks we had when I was a kid and life was simple. Sometimes I'm grateful for the reprieve from her judgment. Tonight, dinner alone would have been welcomed. Instead, I got lectured on everything I can't change.

Getting her to leave didn't take as long as I expected. As soon as she closes the door, I hop up and lock it. My parents hate when I lock the door, but I don't need any more unwelcome interruptions tonight. My bed beckons me, but if I don't do some work and study for my upcoming tests, I'm going to fall further behind. The truth is, I don't want to fail any classes. I want to do well in school. If I didn't care about school, my job, and baseball, I wouldn't be busting my ass every day. Putting in time and effort to do my best is important to me, but I'm at my breaking point. That only makes it worse. Wanting to do well and failing is much harder on my mental state than not caring if I fail.

I need to talk to Izzy. She always makes me feel better, but it's too late tonight. I pull out a piece of paper and pen instead of studying for my tests.

Izzy and I have always written notes to each other

when we need to talk but can't. She leaves hers in a small coffee can in a hole in the tree that she found the day we built the treehouse. I thought about using the can the first time I wrote a letter, but I was ten and really into making paper airplanes. So, the first time I wrote to her, I folded the letter into a plane and sailed it through the window of the treehouse. Izzy was so excited when she found the letter the next day. The paper airplane idea stuck, and now that's how I get every letter to her.

Right now, I desperately need her. When I can't talk to her directly, writing it in a letter helps. I know she'll have some wise advice for me as soon as she reads the letter.

Izzy,

Everything is falling apart. The day got even worse when I went inside. Coach called my parents, and now they're more disappointed in me. They ganged up on me when I was eating dinner and told me how upset they are that I failed my history test and got in trouble with Coach. I tried explaining that I'm overwhelmed, but they won't listen to me. I can't keep this schedule up much longer. Everything needs to stop before I break.

Eli

Once I'm sure my parents are asleep, I quietly sneak downstairs and out the back door. I stop at the table on the porch, fold the letter into an airplane, and walk into the yard. Standing in the perfect spot, I position myself so the plane will sail through the treehouse window that faces Izzy's house. As the paper airplane soars through the air and into the treehouse, my body relaxes, and the stress weighing me down lifts some. Feeling a little better, I return to my room to get some sleep.

chapter
five

The afternoon sun turns the metal building into a sauna as I clean and organize the storage shed behind Bait Your Hook. Dad makes me do this about once a month, so it doesn't get too cluttered. Fishermen tend to toss their gear in here at the end of a long day without bothering to organize anything. It's not a bad job, except for the heat. The building has no air conditioning and very little ventilation. I should be thankful it's February and not July. Plus, it's better than being on the docks with my dad.

Today, he is doing monthly boat inspections. It's a boring job and would be made worse with the constant lecturing from him. I've had enough of that the past few days. I was grateful when he sent me to the storage shed. He probably doesn't want to be around me, either.

Nets, fishing rods, line, lures, and hooks litter the floor. I get to work organizing the larger items first. I place the rods in the large standup bins, then fold nets and shelve them by size. Checking each cooler to make sure they're clean, I'm grateful that none of them have fish remnants or water. The stench of a fishing cooler that sits for days without being washed is horrendous. Once the coolers are stacked against the back wall, I get to work on the smaller items. First, I sweep them into a pile in the center of the room then grab the containers. It's easier to bring the individual containers to the floor and sit in one spot. I open each container and line them up before sitting between them and the tackle pile. I toss the hooks, lures, bobbers, weights, and lines into the correct bins for the next hour. Once the job is done, I store the bins on the shelves and sweep the entire building. By the time I finish, sweat is dripping down my face and back. I pull off my shirt and wipe the sweat from my brow before it drips into my eyes.

The building next door houses the washers and dryers for the marina. Anyone living here, or renting a slip, can use the laundry room. The load I started a couple of hours ago is waiting for the dryer, so I move the towels over and start a second load, tossing my shirt in. Unless it's before eight in the morning, Dad only allows us to use one of the washer/dryer sets so the guests will have access to the other five. If he'd let me use more than one, I could do the laundry in half the time. I understand his point, but we're not busy this time of year, and no one is using the facilities today.

"We don't want guests to wait, and you never know when someone will be ready to wash their clothes." His words echo in my head. I have most of his lectures memorized at this point.

"Yo, Sterling!" someone calls as I exit the laundry room.

I look up to see Bomb, Cap, and Jonesy walking down the dock toward the bait and tackle shop. They must've thought I was on one of the boats. These are three of my closest friends. We've played baseball together for years. Jonesy and I have been on the same team since I started playing when I was eight. Cap is a year older, and Bomb's a senior. We played on the same team on and off through the years until they moved up an age bracket. We've always hung out even when we weren't on the same team.

"Hey, guys." I wave to them and jog over to meet them halfway.

"We're headed to Barnacles. Wanna come?" Jonesy asks.

"Can't. My shift doesn't end for another hour."

"Come on! Can't you blow off the last hour? It's your dad. He won't care," Cap pushes.

"Trust me—he'll care." I'll never hear the end of it if I leave early. "Sorry." I shrug. The guys follow me into Bait Your Hook.

"Seriously, Eli. Let's go," Bomb begs.

"I bet your dad won't even notice you're gone," Cap adds.

"I'm not skipping out early. I can meet you guys there after my shift," I say with finality.

Not only will my dad notice, but I'll be grounded if I leave without permission. Sometimes, I don't even get to leave when my shift ends because he adds on a job at the last minute.

"Hello, boys," my dad greets my friends, coming in from the back office. He drops a file folder on the counter and opens his laptop.

"Hi, Mr. Sterling," my friends respond in unison.

I silently beg them to leave. *Please don't keep badgering me in front of my dad.* Jonesy recognizes the look and motions for our friends to follow him.

"Alright, we'll see you after work," Cap says.

"See ya," I call.

Bomb doesn't budge. He looks right at my dad, and I know he's about to do or say something that's going to get me in trouble.

Please keep your mouth shut.

"Mr. Sterling, how's business?" he asks, sounding like he actually cares.

"Good, son. Really good."

"That's great! You gonna be at the games this year?"

"Wouldn't dream of missing a chance to see my boy play," my dad says with a smile.

Yeah, so you can tell me how much I suck after.

"Excellent," Bomb continues. He smiles, turning on the charm that gets him anything he wants from adults, friends, and girls. "You know, Mr. Sterling, I could use a few pointers on my swing."

What the hell is Bomb saying? He's the best hitter we've got.

My dad beams. "I'd be happy to help," my dad

53

replies. I can't believe he's buying Bomb's bullshit. "Come by any time and we'll work on it."

"Wow, thank you so much, sir." Bomb turns to leave, then pauses and turns back to my dad. "So, Mr. Sterling, do you think Eli could leave a little early today and come hang out with us? You know, talk team strategy and stuff."

Dad looks from my friends to me and back to them. He takes a deep breath and lets it out slowly then looks at the clock. "I guess that will be okay since it's team related. Go ahead with your friends," Dad offers.

"What?" I question in shock. "I have another hour in my shift, and I just started a second load of towels." *Why am I arguing with him?*

"I'll finish the laundry. You go with your teammates."

"Really? Are you sure?" I ask reluctantly.

That doesn't sound like my dad at all. Damn, Bomb really does know how to charm anyone. I've seen it work on girls and teachers, but I never dreamed it would work on my dad.

"I'm sure."

"Cool. Let me grab a shirt. I'll meet you guys outside."

My dad puts his hand on my shoulder as I pass, stopping me. "Their influence might do you some good," he whispers.

There it is—the real reason he's letting me leave early. I'm a screw-up and he thinks my friends can fix me. Well, I've got news for him, they aren't the influence he's expecting. If he knew me at all, he would know that I don't care what my friends do. If I want to be stupid with them, I will. I walk away if I'm not in the mood for their antics. I am capable of being my own person.

Grabbing an extra shirt from the drawer Dad and I keep extras in, I say, "Thanks, Dad," and pull the shirt over my head, following my friends outside. His intentions aren't exactly honorable but calling him out isn't worth the hassle.

At least something good came from Bomb's bullshit. Honestly, I had no idea Dad was in back when I told my friends no. That's probably a good thing. I might have been overly dramatic when telling them no if I knew he was in earshot, although it's unlikely that he heard our conversation. He wouldn't have been so quick to let me go if he heard them trying to convince me to leave without permission.

Barnacles is about a mile away at the south end of the docks. Bomb leaves his truck at Ashton Marina, and we walk down the boardwalk that winds from one end of the island to the other along the Gulf. At the north end of the boardwalk are Ashton Marina, Bait Your Hook, Gulf Charters, several stores, a coffee shop, and a few restaurants. Further down the boardwalk are a few houses with private docks, then miles of public beach before ending at the island's south end, where two smaller marinas, a few shops and Barnacles are located.

Barnacles is your typical beachy restaurant with fried seafood, burgers, and wings. They have televisions set up all around the place and are always crowded anytime there's an NFL or college football game or MLB game. This is the perfect time of year to go—football season is over and baseball season hasn't started.

Walking through the door, the smell of fried food and salty air hits me. Barnacles is an open-air restaurant with three sides screened in. The side that faces the Gulf is completely open with tables outside on the deck and a few in the sand in a roped-off area. They have a bar inside and another outside on the covered deck. You can see one of the thirty TVs from anywhere you sit. Every booth and table is painted a different color. Nothing matches, yet it all goes together to create the perfect décor. We make our way to the far-left side where a green and yellow booth is against the wall. Next to it is a long, rainbow-colored table that seats ten. When it's just the four of us, we take this booth, but when more of the guys from the team join us, we claim the large table. These two tables are far from private, but they are the furthest away from any other tables. We tend to get loud, especially after a win, not that it really matters since Barnacles is never quiet, but we try to be respectful of other patrons. Coach would have us running laps for days if he caught wind of us disrupting families trying to enjoy a meal. Since Ashton Bay is a small town where everyone knows your business, it would take about five seconds for the news to reach Coach. So, there's that.

"Hey, boys," Lindsay purrs, placing a stack of

menus on the table and then sliding in next to Cap.
Lindsay is a junior and has a huge thing for Cap.
According to him, they've hooked up a few times, but
I'm not sure I believe that. Lindsay seems like she's
out for more than a casual roll between the sheets. It's
possible that she wants more because Cap is telling the
truth. He rests his arm around her shoulder and pulls
her in for a kiss. Okay, then. Maybe there *is* a relationship brewing.

Lindsay pulls away, giggling. "Can I get you guys
something else to drink?"

"How 'bout a round of beers," Bomb suggests.

"How about a round of sodas," she counters,
holding his gaze, refusing to waver first.

"That'll work," Bomb concedes.

"I'll have water," I tell her.

"I'll be right back," she says in her cute, Southern
accent before bouncing off toward the kitchen.

"What was that?" Jonesy asks with amusement in
his voice as soon as she's out of earshot.

"What?" Cap feigns innocence.

"You and Lindsay? Really? I thought it was casual?" Jonesy continues.

"It is."

"Casual doesn't kiss like that in public and risk a
different casual seeing it."

Jonesy's argument is on point. No guy our age
who's out to jump from one bed to the next is going to
take a chance of any of his potential one-nighters
seeing him kiss a girl as if they're an item. It's way too
risky.

"It's possible we're considering being a little more than casual," Cap admits.

"Shit. Cap's got a girlfriend!" Bomb broadcasts.

"Shut up," Cap shushes him. "We're just talking. I'm not ready for the universe to know."

"Aww, fuck. Now he's talking about the universe. Next thing you know, he'll be telling us how the stars aligned, the moonlight bounced off her hair, and they fell madly in love," Bomb singsongs the last few words.

"Fuck you," Cap snaps.

"Ooh, testy. Must be *true* love," Jonesy piles on, and we all laugh at Cap's expense.

"She's coming," Cap announces, pleading with his eyes for us to be quiet.

There are still a few chuckles around the table when she arrives, but none of us say anything to her. We're not always complete assholes.

"What can I get you guys to eat?" Lindsay asks, placing our drinks on the table.

"Shrimp basket," Bomb orders.

"Buffalo or regular?"

"Buffalo."

"What side?

"Fries."

She jots down his order and looks at Jonesy next. "Shrimp basket. Regular. Spuds," he orders.

Spuds are these amazing freaking potatoes that are cut into thin ovals, fried then covered with melted cheese. You can get them loaded, too, with things like bacon, green onions, chili, sour cream, and other toppings. They're delicious.

"Cheesy or Loaded?"

"Cheesy."

"What about you?" she asks, looking at me.

"Buffalo fish fingers and cheesy spuds," I answer.

"And what can I get you, sweetheart?" she asks Cap in a flirty tone. She definitely likes him, and by the way he's staring at her, I'd say he feels the same way.

"How about you?" He winks

Barf. She giggles and bats her eyes at him. Barf, again.

"Maybe later," she flirts back.

"I'll hold you to it." Cap winks. "For now, I'll have the oyster basket with slaw."

"Excellent choice." Lindsay giggles again and then bounces off to the next table.

"Excellent choice, sweetheart," Bomb mocks in his best high-pitched voice.

"Shut the hell up," Cap retorts.

"Cap and Lindsay sitting in a tree-" Jonesy sings.

"I will fucking punch you if you finish that song," Cap barks, causing us all to fall over with laughter.

chapter
six

My parents still aren't happy with me, but they are backing off some. Dad cut my hours at the marina. He told me that if I put in a six-hour day on Sundays and still work my four hours on Mondays and Saturdays when a game doesn't interfere, then I don't have to come in on the weekdays before school. Being able to sleep until after seven in the mornings has made a big difference this past week.

Shockingly, I wasn't benched for the first game. Coach talked to my history teacher and convinced him to let me retake the test I failed. I barely passed, but it was enough to keep a low C so I could play. Two weeks into the season and I've managed to keep myself off the bench.

Not working so many hours has afforded me more time to study. I'm slowly bringing my grades up. I'm never going to be an A student, but if I can be a solid C student, my parents might stay off my back. The day-today continues to be a struggle. Even with working fewer hours, I can't seem to shake the feeling of dread that's dragging me down. Baseball has been my escape for years, but it doesn't feel the same as it once did. My major league dreams and getting out of this town are the only things that drive me forward. Is that enough? Every day there's a reason to give up. Every day I want to quit. Every day the events of last April weigh me down.

After my parents went to bed, I grabbed my backpack and laptop and snuck out to the treehouse. It's the only place I find peace. Nothing else matters when I'm up here. Even baseball doesn't seem to exist. My job is a distant memory. School is out of my mind. The only thing that matters up here is Izzy. She's all that exists in the treehouse. Here we are one—our friendship, her artwork, our souls. This is the one place we can be together where no one else exists. We can leave the world behind us.

Izzy won't be here tonight. It's after midnight, so I'm sure she's asleep. Being up here alone late at night doesn't bother me. It's a nice break when Izzy's with me but having some time alone to decompress is good for me, too.

Climbing into the treehouse, I find the nearest wall and slide down it, tossing my backpack on the floor next to me. It's a move I've repeated over and over through the years. Stretching my legs out, I'm inches from the opposite wall. I dread the day I won't fit up here. That's not an option, so I guess I'll have to knock a wall down when that happens.

Before starting my homework, I open a letter from Izzy.

Dear Eli,

Now that soccer season is over, I'll have more free time. It kind of stinks that my season ends right as baseball season starts. Yeah, I know it's been that way for a few years and I should be used to it by now, but I'm not! The one good part is that we can watch each other play since our games don't overlap.

I hope your team makes it to State. That would be so cool. I can't wait to watch you play. You're going to do great this year. I can feel it. You're the best pitcher I've ever watched. Good luck!

Izzy 🩶

She's always encouraging and building me up. I do the same for her. Reading her note makes me feel better. I keep them all in a small, metal box in case I want to reread them later.

It's time to get some work done. Tomorrow, I have tests in math and science, and I have a paper to finish for English. I'm pretty solid at science, so a quick review should be enough. Math is a different story. It will take me longer to review the formulas and make sure I understand the material well enough to get at least a high C or low B. I'll save that for last.

The paper for English is the final project for our unit on *Lord of the Flies* by William Golding. We have to write an essay about one of the themes in the book and how it relates to our life. I chose to write about the loss of innocence and how no matter how sheltered you are or how much your parents try to protect you, there's no going back once something happens that steals your childhood. You can't regain your innocence. Nothing can change the things those boys saw and did on the island. Just like in life, no one can take back a tragedy or trauma. Once it happens, it's embedded deep in your soul and changes the person you were and the person you will become. Tragedy alters the entire course of your life. The paper is good and only needs a few edits. I decide to pull out my laptop and put the finishing touches on it, then I'll review for the science test before studying for the math test. It's a good plan if I can stay awake and focused.

———

The treehouse is too bright. The battery-operated lanterns don't offer this much light. Confusion washes over me as I blink a few times while my brain struggles to catch up. *Shit*. Sunlight peeks through the window. Falling asleep up here was not in my late-night plans. Needless to say, studying for my math test didn't happen. I finished my paper but fell asleep reviewing my science notes. Pressing the button on the side of my phone, 7:42 stares back at me. Shit! I have about thirty minutes to get to school. My parents are going to be livid if they know I didn't sleep in my room. After gathering my stuff, I scramble down the ladder and rush to the back porch. The kitchen is empty, so I quietly open the back door and listen for my parents. Silence. I tiptoe through the kitchen and down the hall to the stairs. I'm almost to the top when my dad's voice startles me.

"What are you doing?"

"Um, nothing. Just going to my room."

Does he know I haven't been here all night? Is he waiting for me to tattle on myself?

"Interesting. I didn't see you in the kitchen. Have you had breakfast?"

What? Where the hell was he? "No, not yet. I'm not really hungry," I lie. "I'm going to go throw on some clothes and head to school."

In an effort to end this conversation, I run up the last few steps, closing the bedroom door behind me.

After changing out of my pajama pants and Marlins shirt and into some jeans and an Ashton Anglers baseball shirt, I rush back downstairs and out the front door. Dad knows I wasn't home last night. Technically, I was home. The treehouse is partially on our property. Doesn't matter. He was baiting me, waiting for me to squeal. If he wants to know where I was, he can ask. Otherwise, I'm not revealing the truth.

The second bell rings as I slip through the classroom door. Made it on time.

"Barely," Coach criticizes. *Not in the mood.*

Instead of saying anything out loud that will end with me running laps, I choose to keep quiet. As I pass a couple of the guys on the team, we exchange high fives and 'what's ups.'

Coach gets started taking roll and going over pointless information that he has to share with us each morning, then he starts the morning announcement video. It's a waste of time. Do we really need homeroom? The daily announcements could be sent in an email or text. None of us would read it, but it's not like anyone pays attention to the video.

My mind wanders to Izzy. I wonder what it's like to be homeschooled. Izzy spends about four hours a day completing school assignments through her online, self-paced classroom then her time belongs to her. She works on her art, visits museums, helps her mom cook, reads, and plays soccer. Sounds like a great life.

Too bad she isn't with me during the day. She would make school so much more bearable. She should be here. Best friends shouldn't be separated for any reason. It isn't fair. The time I have to spend with her has dwindled to a few passing minutes each week in the treehouse. I hate that life has taken this turn, that our relationship has come to this.

"Eli!" someone yells, gaining my attention.

"Huh?" I question, pulling myself back to reality.

"Bell rang," Jonesy tells me.

I look around at an almost empty classroom. Other

than Jonesy and me, all the students have left. Coach is at his desk typing something on his computer.

"Yeah, uh, yeah, I know," I stammer.

"Sure, you did," he laughs.

"You guys coming?" Bomb questions, poking his head into the classroom. His homeroom is next door, and we usually walk to our next classes together.

Bomb is the best hitter we've got. Three years ago, during his freshmen season, he hit seven home runs in three games, earning him the nickname.

"Let's go," I bite.

Today, listening to my friends rag on me is not at the top of my list.

"Cranky," Jonesy teases, following me into the hallway. Turning, I take a step toward him, getting in his face.

"You don't want to push me today," I snap.

"You don't want to start something you can't handle," he returns.

"Wanna bet," I bark, shoving him and causing his back to hit the wall behind him.

He retaliates, taking a step forward and pushing me. "What the hell, Eli?" he yells.

Students gather around us, hungry for a fight. I stumble back a few steps, quickly regaining my footing and getting in his face again.

"That was a mistake."

I raise a fist in one fluid motion and punch him in the nose. Blood spews, splattering our shirts. He staggers backward and hits the wall again. The crowd cheers and hollers, encouraging us to fight. Jonesy pushes himself away from the wall and takes a step toward me. He's tough, I'll give him that.

"What the fuck is wrong with you?" he yells. Jonesy takes a swing at me, but I see it coming and take a small step to the left. His fist hits my shoulder with enough force to knock me back.

Quickly, I move toward him, ready to hit him again, but Bomb steps between us. He puts both hands on my chest, blocking my advances. I fight against Bomb as Jonesy attempts to push past him to get to me. Bomb is strong, but not strong enough to hold us away from one another for long.

"Stop!" Bomb yells. Cap steps behind Bomb and tries to hold Jonesy back while Bomb holds me in place.

A few teachers shove their way through the mass of students.

"Enough!" one of them yells. She looks at Jonesy. "Are you okay?" Jonesy nods. He's not okay—blood pours from his now crooked nose and covers the front of his shirt. It looks bad. "Let's get you to the nurse," she continues, shaking her head at me before escorting Jonesy down the hall.

"What the hell is your problem?" Bomb yells, pinning me with a disappointing glare.

"He was being an ass!" I yell, throwing my hands up as if my statement is explanation enough. Bomb doesn't get a chance to argue before Coach steps up.

"Everybody, get to class!" he bellows over the noise. Kids scramble in every direction. Bomb doesn't budge. I turn to head for my next class, but Coach grabs my arm. "Not you. Go to class, Bomb," he commands. Bomb rushes off. "Let's go," Coach tells me, leading me toward the principal's office. "Do you know how much trouble you're in?"

"Does it matter?" I retort.

"I don't know what the hell is up with you lately, but you better get yourself together, or you'll be off the team?"

"Like that'll happen," I mumble.

"What?" Coach stops, turning to me and giving me a death glare.

"Nothing."

Whether he understood me or was trying to get me to repeat it doesn't matter. He knows I'm right—the team needs me. There's no way they'll go to State with the other pitchers. They're decent but not good enough to take us all the way.

When we walk into the office, Mr. McCaffrey, the principal, is waiting. Word travels fast. Guess it doesn't hurt that the nurse's office is next to the main office.

"Thank you. I'll take it from here," Mr. McCaffrey tells Coach.

Coach leaves and Mr. McCaffrey steps aside, motioning for me to step into his office.

"Have a seat, Eli. Tell me, what happened."

"He got in my face," I grunt out.

"So, you hit Jonesy and probably broke his nose?" he asks.

"He got in my face," I repeat louder.

"Don't yell at me. That's no excuse for what you

did. Your parents are on their way to pick you up. I'm suspending you for three days."

"What? I can't play ball if I'm suspended. The team needs me!" I bark.

"You should have thought about that before you punched someone."

I stand up, slapping my hands on his desk. "Come on! This isn't fair."

"Sit down, Mr. Sterling," he insists firmly.

I don't move, but I speak a little calmer. "Jonesy will be fine. I didn't hit him that hard."

"Sit down, *now*." Before I can move, there's a knock on the door.

"Come in," he calls.

My parents walk into the office full of anger and disappointment. Great. The next three days are going to be hell. I take that seat Mr. McCaffrey keeps insisting on, and my parents sit in the other two chairs. Mr. McCaffrey explains what happened then tells them about my suspension.

"What do have to say for yourself, son?" Dad asks me.

I stare at my dad in response. Nothing I can say will make him happy, get me out of trouble, or make anything about this situation better, so, I keep my mouth shut.

"Answer me!" Dad bellows, standing up and looming over me. He thinks he intimidates me.

"What do you want me to say?" I snap, getting up and standing toe-to-toe with him. "Jonesy got what he deserved, and I'd do it again. Get the fuck off my back."

My dad grabs my arm and pulls me to the door. "Go to the car. I'll deal with you later." He shoves me into the main office.

Instead of going to the car, I wait outside of Mr. McCaffrey's door so I can listen to their conversation. I deserve to know what they say about me.

"Is there anything else we need to do?" Mom asks the principal.

"No. Eli can return on Monday. I'll speak to Coach about how this will affect him playing baseball. He won't be able to play in any of the games before Monday, but Coach might want to add his own punishment since he hit his teammate. Also, you can expect to hear from Jonesy's family. I'm sure there will be doctor bills involved. That will have to be handled between the two families."

"We understand. Thank you," she says in a sickeningly sweet voice, as if being all sugary is going to make this better.

It was stupid of me to hit Jonesy. We've been friends and teammates half our lives. If it hadn't happened at school, he would have made up some lie to tell his parents, and eventually, we both would have calmed down, apologized, and moved forward. Now the school is involved, and my parents will probably have to pay his doctor's bills. Damn.

chapter
seven

"I told you to go to the car," Dad barks when he sees me standing outside the principal's office.

"I decided to wait." I shrug.

"You chose to ignore me and listen to a private conversation."

My parents walk past me and out the door toward the parking lot.

I jog to catch up with them. "It was about me."

My dad stops at the front of his truck and turns. Anger erupts from him, causing me to take a step back.

"If I wanted you to listen, I wouldn't have told you to go to the car," he growls.

I'm not scared of my dad. He's never physically hurt me, and I don't believe he ever will, but I might have gone too far today. I've never seen that level of anger from my father. It's going to be a bad day.

Without another word, my parents climb into the truck. I have two choices—get in or walk home. Right now, my dad probably will prefer if I walk home, but it will likely tick him off if I start to without him telling me to do it. I open the back door and ride with them.

My mom remains completely silent. She hasn't said anything other than being all nice to the principal. Disappointment radiates from her. She won't even look me in the eye.

Don't let them get to you, Eli. Hold your ground. "Jonesy deserved what he got."

"You keep saying that, but no one deserves a broken nose!" Dad barks.

Fuck! I didn't realize I said the last part out loud until my dad called me out.

"He was being an ass," I argue.

"I don't know what's wrong with you, boy," Dad snaps as he pulls onto the main road. "Do you know how serious this is? You hit a teammate. No one should ever hit a teammate. Jonesy is your friend."

"He was in my face," I argue. *Stop talking. Why are you getting him more riled up?*

"You don't have any respect for yourself or your teammates if this is how you treat them."

"I respect my teammates." *Why won't my mouth listen to my brain and just shut up?*

"That's how you show respect to your teammates?" This time I'm smart enough to keep quiet. There's no right response to his question. "Answer me!" he roars, hitting the steering wheel. Mom and I both jump in our seats.

"I-I," I stutter, trying to remember the question.

"No," I finally guess, hoping it's the right response. I hold my breath.

"No. Exactly." Relief washes over me. *One point for Eli.*

My dad pulls into the driveway and puts the car in park. He turns to me while my mom climbs out and goes inside. Guess she doesn't have any input.

"How do you think the rest of the team is going to feel?"

"They-"

"I'll tell you how." Okay. Guess that was a rhetorical question. "They aren't going to trust you. On the field, trust is everything. If your team doesn't trust you, the entire game breaks down."

A little dramatic there, Marcus. The entire game isn't going to break down just because I punched Jonesy. This man is losing his mind.

He gets out but stops by the front of the truck. That must be my cue to get out. I was hoping he would go inside, giving me a chance to sneak off to the treehouse.

"I want you to walk to the marina and help Mike out for the rest of the day."

"What? Why do I have to work?"

"Because you got suspended and aren't going to spend the day relaxing," he snaps.

"Can't I ride with you?"

"No. I'm going to check on your mother. She's upset. You need to leave. Now. I'm texting Mike to let him know you're on the way." He pulls out his phone and starts typing. "He's going to let me know as soon as you arrive, so you better go straight there."

Without another word, Dad walks inside and closes the door. Well, isn't this bullshit just great?

———

The walk to the marina is not nearly long enough to clear my head. Thoughts of disappointing my mom, making my dad angry, hurting my friend, and having to work all afternoon fight for headspace. None of them actually win, and my head is cloudier than when I left my house.

"Eli, my man," Captain Mike calls as I approach the boat.

He's way too excited to see me. I wonder what my dad told him. No matter what Dad says, Mike will have questions. He likes to give me advice about how to handle my dad. Sometimes, I appreciate it because the advice helps me look at the situation differently. Other times, it annoys me because I don't feel like he truly sees my side and is only looking through a father's eyes.

"'Sup, Captain," I grumble. "Where do you need me?"

"Come aboard. I have a charter this afternoon, so I need to get ready for it. Can you make sure everything is stocked while I get the coolers prepped?"

"Sure thing."

Starting in the head, I work my way through the boat, checking towels, supplies, the first aid kit, and snacks. As I work, I make a list on my phone of everything that's missing so I only have to make one trip to the shed. I'm finishing my list when Mike comes in, sets two sodas on the table, and takes a seat.

"Join me," he suggests in a way that tells me not to argue.

Well, this can't be good. The soda makes a hissing sound when I open it, and a little sprays onto my hand and the table. I wipe my hand on my shirt but don't bother to clean the table. Captain Mike raises an eyebrow at me when I remain standing. I roll my eyes, frustrated at this entire day.

"What?" I ask, slumping into the seat across from him.

"Anything you want to talk about?"

Is he kidding me? "No," I bark, getting up.

"Sit down." Well, that's a little firm coming from Mike. He doesn't break eye contact, waiting for me to obey.

"Ugh!" I grunt, dropping back into the seat.

"Talk."

"What do you know?"

"Nope. You tell me what happened."

"I don't know." I shrug. He fixes his glare on me, so I give in. "Jonesy got in my face, and it was like a switch turned on... or off. I don't know. I was so full of rage, and I couldn't stop myself. Once I hit him, all I wanted to do was keep hitting him."

That sounds bad. I didn't consider what I felt in that moment until now. What I told Mike is true. If no one had been there to stop me, I would have kept

75

hitting Jonesy. Damn. That's scary. Why do I feel this way? What is happening to me?

"What did Jonesy say to you when he got in your face?"

My mind replays the morning, but I can't seem to recall what was said. "I can't remember," I whisper. Wow, I hit someone and don't even know why.

"Things didn't go well at home, I take it?"

"What do you think?" I snap.

"Your dad is pretty damn pissed. It takes a lot to get Marcus Sterling mad, but you've gotten him angrier than I've ever seen in all the years I've known him."

"That's why I was exiled to the docks. He couldn't stand to be around me. My mom wouldn't look at me or talk to me," I admit.

"Being exiled to the dock isn't so bad. A day on the water will be good for you," Mike says.

"A day away from my dad will be good for me," I correct.

"Your dad is a good man, Eli. You're taking your anger out on him. It isn't right. He's not the problem. What happened today is *your* fault. The choices you make have consequences."

"I don't need a lecture from you!" I bark, jumping up. I need to get some fresh air. Mike grabs my arm as I pass.

"You are going to listen," he states calmly, rising to meet my eyes. "I know the past ten months have been hard on you, but making these bad choices has to stop. If your dad was out of line, I would tell you. There's no denying that. I've done it before. But he's not the one who screwed up today. You are. You were out of line when you hit your friend, and I'd venture to guess you said some things to your dad that were out of line, too."

Mike's words play around in my head. He's right. My dad was right. Mr. McCaffrey was right. I screwed up. Big time. That's not something I'm ready to admit out loud. I don't like being wrong or admitting my mistakes. I will, but I need time. There's still too much anger bubbling at the surface ready to boil over, and I don't want to take it out on Mike, or anyone else.

"Finish your tasks. I'm going to grab us some lunch from Barnacles. We'll have time to eat before the charter guests arrive."

chapter
eight

By the time Mike gets back, I've finished everything on my list. He hands me a bag of food and a bottle of water.

"I'm going to eat in the cockpit so I can do my final check," he tells me.

"Alrighty." Good, that will give me some time to myself.

"We pull out at one," he reminds me.

Mike heads inside while I climb the ladder to the top deck. I check my phone. We have an hour before the guests arrive. That gives me time to relax after I eat my lunch. I open the bag and unwrap my sandwich —tuna salad on wheat. Nice. There's a bag of chips and a chocolate chip cookie in the bag, too.

As soon as I'm done inhaling my lunch, I pull off my shirt and lie on my back with my hands behind my head. This much-needed free time will give me the chance to do a little soul searching. Mike's right. The past ten months have been hell. Every day, I force myself to get out of bed and muddle through. Some days aren't as tough as others, but none of them are easy. Baseball helps, but it isn't the break from reality that it once was. At one time, playing ball would make everything better. No matter how bad I felt, or what was going on off the field, baseball would change my mood. That hasn't happened in months. Now, baseball is one more thing on my to-do list. It's become another form of stress. School, baseball, home, and work all stress me out. I can't focus long enough to do anything well. Everything makes me miserable. More than anything, I want to be happy. I want to feel good about... something.

Being a constant disappointment to my parents is weighing on me. I want to make them proud, but nothing I do works. My sisters don't talk to me. My friends annoy me. Coach tolerates me because I win games. *Stop wallowing, Eli. You suck. Deal with it and move on. You can't change anything.*

Before I'm ready, voices fill the air. Ugh! Now, I have to go to work. Pushing myself up. I venture a look over the side. Great. Walking toward the boat is a family of six—mom, dad, and their four kids who all look to be under ten. This is going to be a nightmare, especially if this is their first Gulf excursion.

I don't bother putting on my shirt. It's warm today, and I'll be more comfortable without it. Mike will be annoyed because it isn't professional to go shirtless on the job. Dad's words, not Mike's, but he follows all my dad's stupid rules.

When I get to the lower deck, Mike is helping the

family board the boat. He gives me a dirty look but doesn't comment on my missing shirt.

"Meet Melissa and Doug Cranton," Mike hisses. "This is Eli. He'll be helping us today," Captain Mike introduces us.

"Nice to meet you," I say, shaking their hands.

"Nice to meet you, too," Mr. Cranton responds.

"These are our children," Mrs. Cranton starts. "Sarah, Jennifer, Michael, and Thomas."

"Hi," I say. I don't know how to talk to kids, and Mike is having a conversation with the dad. "Um, I'll grab life jackets," I offer.

It doesn't take long to gather life jackets for everyone. I rarely wear one, but passengers are required by Ashton Marina rules to wear one at all times. I drop the kid's vests on the deck and hand one to each parent. Then I face one of the girls.

"Can I help you put on your life jacket?"

She nods silently and takes a tentative step toward me. Poor kid looks terrified. Is she unsure about me or being on the boat? Probably both. I pull the jacket over her head and secure it tightly. By the time I'm finished, Mr. Cranton has his vest on and is securing one for his other daughter. Mrs. Cranton is fighting a screaming Thomas, who looks to be about three. It isn't going well for her. I pick up the other jacket and walk over to Michael. He tries to run from me, but his dad catches him, holding him still while I secure the jacket. Mrs. Cranton is finished with Thomas' jacket by the time we're done. This is going to be impossible. We'll be lucky to get back home with all four kids.

Mike instructs our passengers to sit while we leave the dock. Once everyone is safely seated, I jump onto the dock, untie the boat, and hop back on. Mike starts the engine and expertly guides us away from the dock.

"It's going to be a long afternoon," I tell Mike, joining him in the cockpit.

"They aren't so bad."

"Aren't so bad? Those kids are too young to be on this boat, especially the boys."

"The parents are going to have to pay close attention," Mike agrees.

"How are they going to fish and watch four kids?"

"I don't know, but it's our job to make sure they have a good time even if it makes our day hell."

"Well, isn't that fantastic?" I quip sarcastically.

"It might do you some good to do something nice for someone else. I wouldn't push any buttons if I were you."

Asshole. "Aye, aye, Captain." I salute Mike before going back outside. Being with the family might be better than dealing with him.

On the deck, the oldest girl, Sarah, I think, is sitting quietly as Mike instructed. The other girl, I can't remember her name, is puking in a bucket. Freaking great. Mrs. Cranton is helping soothe her daughter. Mr. Cranton is trying to wrangle the boys who are running wild around the deck. This is not what I signed up for today. Everything about this should qualify as punishment for hitting Jonesy, getting suspended, and all future infractions.

"This was a mistake," Mrs. Cranton blurts out as I approach her.

"Can I help?" *What? Why did I offer to help?*

She looks at her husband with sadness and desperation. He has Thomas in one arm, holding him like a football, and Michael by the back of the shirt. He nods agreement to his wife.

"We need to turn back. This isn't going to work. I don't know what we were thinking."

"Oh, yeah, I guess that will be okay. Let me talk to Captain Mike."

"Thank you."

A thought hits me as I reach the door to the cabin. "Hey, if it helps, your family can sit inside the cabin until we get back to the dock."

"Yes, that will be great. Thank you so much," Mr. Cranton calls with relief.

"You take the boys. I'll sit out here with the girls," his wife offers.

Mr. Cranton follows me inside with Thomas and Michael. After getting them settled with some snacks and drinks, I seek out Mike.

"So, the kids are a nightmare," I whisper to Mike. "The family wants to go back to port. Their kids are out of control."

"Are you sure?"

"Yeah. The dad is inside with the boys so no one goes overboard, and the mom is outside. They've got one girl puking and the other is surprisingly sitting still."

Mike shakes his head at me. "I told them it was a

bad idea when they booked the trip, but they wouldn't listen. Apparently, Doug insisted on fishing during this vacation."

"He could have fished off the pier."

"Told him," Mike confirms. "Tell them we're headed back and should be docked in about forty-five minutes."

An hour later, we're docked, and the family is sitting at a picnic table outside the bait shop eating ice cream. What a waste of time. At least I didn't have to teach the kids how to fish. They probably would have ended up hooking each other instead of the fish. It didn't take long to help Mike prep the boat for the next day since we didn't use much of anything. I clean the mess the boys made with their snacks, then hose down the deck while Mike gasses up the boat and empties the ice in the coolers.

"Damn, boy. Did you use sunscreen?" he asks, coming up behind me and poking my shoulder.

"What?" I ask, looking over my shoulder.

"You're burned."

"No way. I wasn't out there long."

"Did you have your shirt off during lunch?"

"Yes."

"That was almost three hours ago."

It doesn't hurt. Maybe Mike is wrong. I risk a look at my arms and chest. *Shit*. I am red. "It's bad, isn't it?"

"Yeah, it's going to hurt by tonight. You need some serious aloe." He walks into the cabin and returns seconds later with a bottle of green goo. "Do you want me to put some on your back?" he offers.

"Sure, thanks."

Mike lathers my back with after-sun lotion before handing the bottle to me. I do the same to my arms and chest. The next few days are going to be miserable. How could I be so stupid?

chapter
nine

By the time I get home, it's after nine. Mike and I finished early since the charter didn't work out, but I volunteered to stay and keep working. I spent the afternoon helping other captains with their haul as they returned to the docks then took my sweet time prepping the boats for tomorrow. It was still early, so I washed, dried, and folded all the towels. I could have left those for the morning, but the thought of coming home filled me with dread. When I couldn't find any more work to do, I went for a five-mile run on the beach. Anything was better than going home.

My mom is already upstairs for the night. If she didn't go to bed early every night, I would think she was avoiding me. Hell, she probably is. Sitting in the truck this morning with my mother's silence drove me insane. She always talks to me whether she's mad, sad, happy, or angry. It doesn't matter what I do, or if she agrees with me, Mom will talk about it. Her silence reeked of disappointment.

My dad sits on the couch, drinking a beer and watching TV. Spending the day on the boat with Captain Mike and then making a point to help the other captains as they returned to the marina kept me from running into my father. I'm eternally grateful for the reprieve. I know how Dad feels about me hitting Jonesy. He made his opinion very clear.

"Your plate is in the oven," he says without looking at me. *Nice to see you, too.*

"Thanks."

The plate is piled high with spaghetti and meat-balls. After seafood, it's one of my favorite meals. Figures my mom would make a meal I love when I'm having had a bad day. It never mattered why we had a bad day, she always fed us until we felt better. It worked great until my sisters became teenagers and started worrying about everything they ate and how it might make them fat. It still works for me. Even in her disheartened state, she took the time to show she cares. The gesture makes me feel a little better.

I had plenty of time to think on the boats and during my run. Jonesy didn't deserve what I did to him. He's a good friend, and I shouldn't be taking my anger out on him, or anyone else. Lately, I've been having a hard time controlling my temper. I knew it would boil over at some point, but I couldn't find a way to stop myself. Too bad it wasn't someone I dislike.

I quickly inhale the pasta so I can get to my room for the night. I'm not fast enough. As I'm putting my dishes in the dishwasher, my dad strolls into the kitchen. He takes another beer from the refrigerator and sits at the table. After checking to make sure there's soap in the little compartment, I turn the dishwasher on, set it for a two-hour cycle, close the door, and press start. Hoping my dad just came in for another beer, I turn for the stairs.

"Not so fast, son."

Ugh! No such luck.

"Sit down," he instructs.

Why couldn't he come in and talk while I ate? I do as I'm told, knowing I don't have much of a choice. I'm in enough trouble. No need to add to it.

"Coach called."

"I know. He texted me. I'm benched for two games after my suspension is over. That's four games. It going to ruin our season if we lose all of them."

"You should have thought about that before you hit Jonesy."

"Well, it doesn't matter now, does it?" I bite out.

"I don't like your attitude. What is wrong with you?"

"Nothing. Can I go to bed? I'm tired." *And I don't want to talk to you about anything important.*

"Have you checked on Jonesy?"

"No. Bomb texted and said his nose is broken. He'll be out for at least two weeks, maybe longer."

"You need to call him and apologize."

"Apologize? For what? He got what he deserved."

"I'm tired of hearing you say that. No one deserves a broken nose. Even when you're angry, violence is never the way to handle any situation."

"How can you say that? You weren't there. You have no idea what he said."

"Oh, this ought to be good," Dad says sarcastically. "Enlighten me. What did Jonesy say that warranted a broken nose?"

Shit. How exactly did I get myself here? The truth is—Jonesy didn't say anything that should have made me so angry. I honestly don't know why I got that mad.

"Tell me!" Dad bellows.

"Um, he, uh, he said I was being cranky and couldn't take him."

"You can't be serious." I simply shrug a response. It's the truth. What else can I say? "So, you punched him for no reason."

"I guess."

Dad shakes his head at me. "Your mother and I talked about your punishment."

"Punishment? Being suspended and benched isn't enough? You're going to add another punishment? I thought you couldn't be punished for the same crime more than once."

"In this house, I can punish you as many times as I want for the same infraction. You're grounded for one month. School, baseball, and work. No friends. No parties. You'll also be paying Jonesy's medical bills."

"Did his parents say we had to pay?"

"I haven't spoken to his parents. I'm going to call them tomorrow and offer for you to pay them. *You.* Not me."

"That's bullshit."

"Language."

"Why would you offer to pay? They might not even ask for money."

"It's the right thing to do. You messed up, and you need to pay for your mistake. It's no different than getting in an accident that's your fault. You're expected to pay for the damages."

"But I need the money I make at the marina. I work hard for it."

"And you'll be working the rest of this week. You won't have school or baseball, so I expect you to be at the marina every morning at seven through Sunday. You will work twelve-hour days for the next four days."

"What? Don't I get a break?"

"No. Getting suspended is not a vacation. At least you'll be making money. If it was a true punishment, I wouldn't pay you for the work."

Standing abruptly, the chair clatters to the floor, and a piece from the back flies across the room. I stomp out of the kitchen like an immature child, not caring about the chair.

"Pick up the chair!" Dad yells. Ignoring him, I rush out of the kitchen. He's right behind me when I reach the stairs. "Where are you going?"

"To bed. I'm done."

"Seven a.m., son. Don't be late."

I'm surprised he let me go that easily. Taking the stairs two at a time, I get to my room as fast as possible and slam the door. This day needs to end. I can't take it any longer. Not bothering with a shower, I fall into bed. Should I text Jonesy? He's probably already asleep.

It's the right thing to do, Eli. Jonesy is your friend. You need to make sure he's okay. On the other hand, he probably doesn't want to hear from me. Right now, he's likely planning his revenge. *Text him. No, give him some time.* I'm so confused and the conflicting thoughts aren't helping.

A silent war wages in my head as I try to decide what to do. My dad didn't need to tell me to apologize to Jonesy. I know that's what has to happen. Picking up my phone, I decide to take the leap. A text is a start.

> Me: Hey. Sorry I broke your nose.

> Jonesy: It sucks. I'm out for at least two weeks.

> Me: I heard. How ya feeling?

> Jonesy: Right now, pretty damn good. The doc gave me some wicked pain meds.

> Me: Get some sleep.

Not waiting for another text, I silence my phone and toss it to the other side of the bed. Jonesy isn't the type to hold a grudge. Next week, it will be like this never happened. I roll over and pull the blanket over me, hoping I can silence my brain long enough to get some rest.

chapter
ten

This week hasn't been any better than last. Since my suspension almost two weeks ago, Coach has made practice hell for me. He's been on my case about everything from the way I pitch and hit to my attitude. Well, if he wasn't being such an asshole, maybe I wouldn't have a bad attitude. He's made me run laps every night for an hour after practice. Cramping in my legs woke me up twice last night. This morning, I'm so sore I can barely move. My entire body is screaming in pain.

We have a game tonight and a doubleheader tomorrow. I'm pumped to get back on the field. I've already missed four of the first seven games this season. It sucks not being able to play. Coach wouldn't even let me sit on the bench when I was suspended. He said that since I was suspended, I wasn't allowed on campus for any reason. What a stupid rule! It's bad enough that I had to sit out, but not being there to support my teammates sucked even worse. Instead, I spent the time busting my ass at the marina.

Making my way out of the locker room to join my teammates on the field for warmups, Coach stops me.

"Sterling, wait a second."

"What's up, Coach?"

"Look, I've thought a lot about your attitude and suspension. I've decided to let Sam pitch tonight."

"What?" I yell. What the fuck is he doing? How can he bench me again? Why do I keep getting punished for the same thing?

"You need to change your attitude and start acting like you're part of the team. Show me you deserve to be on the mound, and I might put you there tomorrow," he says with finality and walks away, leaving me completely dumbfounded.

This can't be happening. The sound of vibrating metal echoes through the empty locker room as my glove hits the opened locker causing the door to slam shut. Leaving the glove where it landed, I kick the locker closest to me a few times while cursing Coach's name.

"Asshole. He can't fucking bench me again!" My yell echoes through the empty locker room.

Scouts are going to start showing up at the games soon. I need to be on the field where they can see what I can do. It might not officially matter until next year, but they'll remember I didn't play.

"Fuck!" I scream, slamming another locker door.

Once I've calmed myself down, I pick up my glove

and head for the dugout. There's no reason to stretch since my ass is going to be on the bench all night. As pissed off as I am at Coach, I have to do what he says if I ever want to be on that mound again.

"You calm?" Coach asks, resting his foot on the bench next to where I'm sitting.

"I guess."

"Why aren't you stretching?" Is this man mental?

"You benched me again," I bark.

"You don't listen. I said you aren't pitching. I never said you aren't playing."

"What?" I consider what Coach just told me.

He's right. I got so angry about being told I'm not pitching that I didn't hear what Coach meant. There are plenty of games I don't pitch. Coach is required to follow state guidelines and rest his pitchers for a certain number of days after pitching. During those games, I play other positions.

Coach stares down at me while I process the conversation, waiting impatiently for me to catch up.

"Stretch!" he finally barks when I don't move.

"Yes, Coach."

My feet carry me to the outfield where our team is stretching and warming up. This might not be so bad. I won't be on the mound where I belong, but at least I'm back on the field.

———

Sam pitched a decent game. *I* would've pitched a no-hitter, but at least we won. It wasn't pretty, but a win's a win. Doing as Coach requested, I encouraged the team and even told Sam he pitched a good game. Hopefully, it was enough to convince Coach to let me pitch tomorrow.

It was after nine by the time I got home. I changed, then made an appearance downstairs and told my parents that I was going to bed early. Once it was safe, I snuck out and met some of the guys at Local Burger Joint, or LBJ as we refer to it. They have the best burgers in Florida. After stuffing ourselves, we went to Bomb's house. His parents have a huge house on several acres of land between my street and the school. There's a long, winding dirt road that leads to their house with at least a hundred trees on the property. It's pretty secluded, but I can see their dock from ours.

Bomb's parents don't care what he does as long as it's in the pool house, where he moved last summer. It's basically a two-bedroom house that he has all to himself. Must be nice to move out of your parents' home and have freedom and privacy. Behind the pool house, there's a covered dock. We've had some awesome parties there over the past year. Tonight, it was more subdued than normal. There was plenty of drinking, but no one ended up in the water. Usually, someone either falls in or gets pushed. Sometimes it's in the pool, sometimes it's in the sound. The water is too cold this time of year to swim by choice, but that doesn't mean no one will end up there. I had a couple of beers but wasn't really in the mood to get plastered.

When I get home, I climb the ladder to the treehouse instead of going to my room. It's dark and quiet. Everyone in the neighborhood is asleep at this hour. Not bothering with the lamp, I find a comfortable position and close my eyes. A pillow and blanket would be a welcome addition up here and make this hardwood floor more comfortable. Good thing I'm wearing a sweatshirt. Temperatures dipped into the forties tonight, but by game time in the morning, it will be in the sixties and will likely creep into the low eighties for game two. I hate this time of year when the range in temperature is so drastic from morning to night. I'll take the sweltering summer heat any day. At least I know what to expect.

Sleep is a must if I'm going to be worth a shit tomorrow, but I'm still wide awake at two. Usually, I come to the treehouse if I'm having trouble sleeping, and it relaxes me. I guess I'll try my bed tonight.

———

Mom made me a protein and carb-filled breakfast like she does every time we have a doubleheader. We don't eat between games, so a big breakfast helps keep the hunger at bay through both games.

The field at Clayton is the worst one in our division. The locker rooms and dugouts are ancient. The visitors' dugout no longer has a roof and the bases need replacing. To top it off, the field is on the main road. Bomb hit a homerun there last season, and the ball hit a passing car. The driver didn't stop, but it had to have damaged the roof. Good thing these are the only two games we play at Clayton this year.

Coach pulls me aside as we exit the bus.

"You're pitching the first game. Mitch is pitching game two. I expect you to wear Clayton out, so Mitch has an easy win."

"You got it, Coach."

I know what Coach means. Mitch is decent and has the potential to be great, but he's a freshman and his arm needs some work. If Clayton is on their game, Mitch can't win against them. In game one, it's up to me to make sure the boys are exhausted. That means letting their strong players get some hits, then getting them out at second or third so they don't score. It isn't an easy feat.

On the mound for only the second time, this season is surreal. My parents are in the stands, my friends are on the field — it's going to be a good day.

The first batter comes to the plate. I eye him cautiously. He's new to Clayton, and his stats say he's good. I throw a fastball first. He swings. Strike One. Second pitch is a little softer. He hits it over my head, but it lands on the ground behind second base and rolls into the outfield. Cap picks it up as the Clayton guy rounds first.

"Come on, Cap. Get it to second." Cap throws the ball. Bomb is ready at second with his glove outstretched and one foot on the base. He catches it as the Clayton player slides towards second and swipes him out.

"That's the way, Sterling," Coach encourages from the dugout.

'Wear them out,' I remind myself. *'But don't exhaust your team in the process.'*

Several more pitches, several more runs to second and third. Three outs, no runs. Not a bad start to the game. A few innings like this and we'll be set.

chapter
eleven

We pummeled Sapsville twelve to two today, which is cause for a huge celebration. Sitting comfortably at ten and one eleven games into the season is a good feeling. Not as good as me being back on the field with my team and my dad deciding that my exemplary behavior deserves early release three weeks into my month-long grounding. The only game we lost was the second game when I was benched. Mitch pitched a great game against Clayton last week. I only allowed two runs in the first game and Mitch allowed three. His game is definitely improving.

Bomb's house is stocked with plenty of beer and liquor. I don't know how he gets his hands on it. It doesn't matter as long as it's free and there's plenty to go around. Coach would kill us if he knew we were partying. He gives us a ten o'clock curfew during the season, but no one adheres to it. Coach is probably asleep in his old man recliner long before ten, so we don't have to worry about him finding out. Even if we do get caught, he can't bench the entire team.

Music vibrates the small house as wall-to-wall bodies move to the beat, drinking, dancing, and making out. Everyone's in motion. After grabbing another beer, I stumble outside. It's getting too hot and crowded in that cramped space. Every kid from our school must be here. It's insane.

I make my way over to a few of the guys from the team. I would hang with Jonesy and Bomb, but Bomb spends most of these parties in his room with whatever girl he's banging. It changes every few weeks, so it's anyone's guess who he's with tonight.

Jonesy hasn't been hanging around me much since I broke his nose. I can't blame him, but it sucks. Tension is high on and off the field when we're near each other. The whole team feels it, and Coach told us both to get over it. Not that simple, but okay, Coach.

I managed to screw up a childhood friendship in a few seconds. Ironically, we had a conversation the week prior about my anger issues and how hot-headed I've been this past year. He was right, and I promised him I'd work on it. I lied. It doesn't matter to me if he thinks I have anger issues. If people don't like me, that's their problem, not mine.

"'Sup, man?" Kyle, the first baseman, high-fives me.

"Good game," Milt, our shortstop, compliments. Damn right it was a good game.

"Thanks," I respond, raising my cup to them before downing the rest of it.

Glad to see a keg out here so I don't have to wade through the crowd inside. I help myself to another beer. This is five, I think. I've lost count at this point. Good thing I told my dad I was crashing here. The truth is, I'll most likely stumble my way home and pass out in the treehouse.

I watch my so-called friends making moves on girls, drinking themselves silly, and hyping each other up. Why are they all such douchebags? Am I like them? Anger builds inside me while I watch from a distance. Why am I at this party? There's no real reason to be here other than a few free beers. I need Izzy with me. I wish she could be here tonight. She always calms me—my nerves, my anger, my anxiety. Whatever the issue, Izzy's presence always makes everything better, but she doesn't like these parties. I brought her to a few last year. She was miserable, so she stopped coming with me.

Looking across the patio, I see Stoner dancing with Leah Randall. Leah and I had a thing in eighth grade for a few months. I don't care who's she with now, but Stoner's a jerk, and well, a stoner. She turns her back to him and grinds against him. Stoner reaches around and takes a tit in each hand. They might as well be screwing right there in front of everyone. Why am I watching them? I shake my head and turn to refill my cup.

"You got a problem?" My cup is knocked out of my hand as the culprit turns me toward him.

"What the fuck was that about?" I yell in Stoner's face.

"You're staring at my girl. No one should be staring at what's mine."

"If you don't want anyone staring, then don't fuck her on the dance floor."

"What did you say?" he grabs me by the front of my shirt.

"Stop, stop." Jonesy and Cap appear next to me.

"Leave him alone. He's drunk," Cap tells Stoner, but I'm not drunk. He lets go of my shirt, and I stumble backward. Okay, maybe I *am* a little drunk.

"He wants my girl."

"He doesn't want Leah," Jonesy counters.

Stoner laughs. "That's right. He's hung up on that little homeschool freak, Izzy."

Rage explodes through my veins. Lunging toward Stoner, I push Jonesy and Cap out of my way. My fist makes contact with Stoner's chin, sending him to the ground. I jump on top of him, getting in three good hits before he rolls us over and lands a right hook to my eye and another to my mouth, busting my lip open. It takes six guys to break up the fight.

Sam, Cap, and Jonesy pull me away while three guys push Stoner in the opposite direction. Leah shakes her head at me and wipes a single tear before following them. *Dramatic*. Why is she upset with me? He started it.

"You need to go home, Eli," Bomb insists, appearing next to me. I guess the commotion interrupted his latest conquer.

"You're kicking me out of your party?"

"He's not kicking you out. You're bleeding. Come

101

on, I'll drive you home and get you cleaned up," Cap offers.

"Nah, I can walk." I shove past my friends and through the crowd, then stalk to the front of the house. They call from behind me, but I don't stop. No one follows me. As soon as I reach the dirt road, I start jogging. I need to put distance between myself and that party as fast as possible.

My mind races as I jog home. Why did that jerk say I'm hung up on Izzy? He doesn't know anything about her or me. No one gets away with disrespecting Izzy. I'll do anything to protect her and her reputation. I'm glad I hit that asshole.

My head spins a little, probably from the beer, not being hit. I can't afford a concussion. There's no way he hit me hard enough to cause that kind of injury. My stomach rolls about the time I reach my street. Jogging after all that beer wasn't the best decision, but I needed to get away from the party.

Good thing the fight wasn't at school. Hopefully, Stoner will keep his mouth shut. I can't afford to miss any more games with scouts showing up to them now. It's too early for me to be scouted for college or the majors, but if they notice me now, they'll be back next year and the year after. On the other hand, if the scouts get wind of any trouble or a shitty attitude, they won't be watching me at all.

Even though my soft, comfortable mattress would help me sleep better, the treehouse beckons me. Skipping the rotted third step, I climb the ladder. That peg needs to be fixed before someone gets hurt.

The floor isn't the best place for me to sleep, but if my parents hear me coming in this late, they'll ask questions. No reason for them to know I'm home.

chapter
twelve

It's still early when I force myself to move. The hard, wooden floor of the treehouse wasn't the best sleeping option after a fight. Plus, I'm hungover. My head pounds as my stomach rolls. How much did I drink? Practice is going to suck today. I've got three hours to recover before I have to be at the fieldhouse. Water and carbs, maybe some Gatorade, should do the trick.

Opening the back door, the smell of waffles and bacon hits me. Walking into the kitchen, I force down bile and pretend everything's good.

"Morning, Mom."

"Good morning, Eli. You're home early," my mom responds, not looking up from the eggs she's scrambling.

"I've got practice in a few hours, so I wanted time to shower and eat."

"Breakfast will be ready in about ten minutes if you want to take a quick shower before you eat."

I keep my head down as I pass her. "Sounds good."

I rush upstairs and start the shower, peeling off my clothes while the water gets hot. I forced myself to keep it together longer than I thought possible. As soon as the door closes, I hurl all over the shower floor and my feet. It takes a few minutes for me to empty my stomach. I wash the mess down the drain and bathe myself. I feel better at the moment. Hopefully, some food will help, too. Once I'm out of the shower, I take some aspirin and dry off. The biggest advantage to having two sisters is getting the bedroom with a private bathroom. They shared the one between their two rooms, and I got my own. It was nice not having to share or deal with all their makeup and crap.

I risk a look in the mirror. Damn. My lip is swollen, and there's a split on the bottom that's already scabbed over. I also have a bruise on the left side of my face near my eye. It isn't bad, and I can see fine, but there's no covering the damage. My parents are going to lose their shit.

"Eli! Breakfast is ready," my mom calls as I'm zipping my jeans. Walking down the stairs, I pull on a t-shirt.

"Oh, Eli, what happened to your face?" Mom asks with concern as soon as she sees me. Dad's head pops up from his phone where he's probably reading a news report.

"Another fight, son?" Dad snaps.

"It wasn't my fault."

"Never is."

"Dad, please listen." If Stoner keeps quiet, I can

make up any reasonably believable story. "Some guys who aren't on the team showed up at Bomb's. They were drunk and causing problems. I got hit a couple of times when we were trying to get them off Bomb's property."

The first part is true. Stoner and Leah aren't on the baseball team, they were both drunk, and Stoner caused the problem. *Please believe me.* I don't want to be grounded again.

"Did you think to call the police and let them handle the situation?" Dad asks, gruffly.

Yeah, right. Even if my story was true, the police would not have been called.

"We handled it. There's was no reason to involve the police."

"Fine. As long as you didn't start something. I better not find out you're lying."

"I'm telling the truth, Dad." *Mostly*.

Satisfied with my story, he nods his head and picks his phone up. *Nice save*. Now, if no one squeals on me, I'll be golden.

Breakfast looks good. Waffles and bacon are two of my favorite breakfast foods. I usually look forward to Saturday and Sunday mornings when my mom cooks a huge meal. Today, not so much. I start with a waffle to see if my stomach can handle it. I need to be careful to eat enough to keep my parents from questioning me, but not so much that it makes me sick again. There is a strategic balance that comes with keeping a hangover a secret during weekend breakfasts with my parents. It's an art I've mastered over the past year.

"How was the rest of your night? Did you boys enjoy watching movies at Bomb's house?" *Oh, Mom, your naivety is so cute.*

"Uh, yeah, you know us. A night full of horror flicks and junk food." Does she really believe this crap?

"Good, son. I'm glad you boys are keeping your noses clean, especially during baseball season," Dad adds.

"Absolutely," I agree.

My stomach feels much better after a second waffle, so I risk a few pieces of bacon. Thankfully, the bacon stays down. I place my empty plate in the sink and grab a Gatorade.

"Thanks for breakfast."

"You're welcome, dear."

"Practice starts at eleven. Can I borrow your truck?"

"Sure. I'm not planning to go to the marina today. If something comes up, I can take Mom's car."

"Thanks." Wow, I can't believe that worked. Sometimes he's good about letting me use the truck. Other times, he acts like I still a kid and can't be trusted to drive the short distance to school.

With an hour left before I need to leave, I set my alarm and lay down on my bed. I doubt I'll fall asleep, but I don't want to take any chances. Being late to a game will be disastrous,

Getting my driver's license should have been life-changing and given me more freedom, but my parents won't buy me a car. I have to share the truck with my dad, which means one of my parents has to drive me most of the time. My other options are bumming rides from a friend or walking to school, which I prefer. I hate depending on other people. If my sister wasn't planning a wedding, they could afford it, but Molly's wedding is more important than anything else. If Emma gets a ring soon, I won't be getting a car next year, either. A car is a necessity. Does Molly really need some big, over-the-top wedding?

Scrolling through my phone, I find pictures on social media from the party—a bunch of drunk kids trying to get laid. As I search through the pictures, I find several of me fighting Stoner. There aren't any of me actually hitting him, but there are a few of me getting in his face and two of us both bloody afterward. Well, shit. There's incriminating evidence against me all over social media. By now, those pictures have probably been shared a hundred times. Let's hope none of them find their way to Coach. I can't afford for him to find out about the fight or the party.

chapter
thirteen

It's been almost impossible, but I've managed to play the good boy for almost two weeks. I haven't gotten in trouble again or been benched. That's a good thing. There was a scout from a minor league team at the game last week, and after he saw me pitch, he asked to meet me even though I'm only a sophomore. He said he liked what he saw and that he'll be following my high school career. If I don't keep my grades up and stay off the bench, he won't be watching for long. I need all the points I can get before senior year if I'm going to have a chance at the majors. I don't want to start in the minors, but I might not have an option. So, I need to be nice to every scout I meet.

Pitching is the position I'm best at, but Coach uses me as a utility player. He plays me when I'm not pitching, giving me the opportunity to work on my skills at other positions. Scouts look for well-rounded players. I'm pretty good at the bases, but the outfield sucks.

Even though center field is my best position after pitching, I hate it. Coach likes me there because of my arm. If someone gets a good hit, I'll be able to get the ball back to the baseman for an out.

If we're not playing a decent team, I can spend half the game at center doing nothing. I suck as a catcher. Coach tried to play me at catcher last year, but it proved to be a disaster. I can catch at the bases and in the outfield, but not behind the plate. I'm fast, too, and can hit pretty good. I can't hit like Bomb—no one can hit like him. He's already been offered scholarships to three D1 schools, and several major league teams are looking at him. He hasn't made his final decision, but I bet he'll enter the draft this summer. He's the only senior on our team with a chance at the majors.

The locker room is loud as the team gets pumped for the game. Coach always has us here an hour early so he can give his pep talk, and we can warm-up. Stretching is a must if we don't want to cramp up or hurt ourselves on the field.

Bomb and I gather up some gear so we can hit a few practice balls. Jonesy usually warms up with us, but he's still keeping his distance. He was slowly warming back up to me before the fight at Bomb's party last week, but he's barely spoken to me since that night.

Tonight, I'm pitching again. We haven't had a game in seven days, so I was able to pitch last Thursday and again today, but I won't be able to pitch Saturday. The team we're playing is one of the toughest we play, so I'll likely throw a lot of pitches.

My arm will need the rest. Last year when we played Central, our pitcher threw close to eighty pitches, which sucked, because it was the first game of a tournament, and he couldn't pitch the rest of the weekend. Don't get me wrong, I get it. It's important to take care of my arm if I'm going to play in the majors, but not being able to pitch multiple games sucks, especially when we play good teams back-to-back.

My mind is running all over the place as I warm up with Bomb. I need to get my head in the game, or my pitching is going to suffer. I throw a ball to Bomb, but it doesn't even reach him. Damn, I hope no one was paying attention. Bomb picks up the ball, but instead of throwing it back to me, he jogs out to the mound.

"What the hell is wrong with you?" he asks in a whisper so no one else can hear.

"Don't know."

"You better figure it out before game time."

"Yeah, yeah. I will." It's a lie, and by the look on Bomb's face, he knows it. "I will! Now go so I can pitch to you again."

"How 'bout you throw something I can hit."

Dick.

When Bomb is back at home plate, I take a few calming breaths, focus on my target, and let the ball soar. Bomb misses, not because the ball fell short, but because he swung and missed. *Strike.* I throw three more balls before he finally hits one. Nice! Now I'm ready to play. I go easy when I'm warming up, saving my fast pitching for the game. It's nothing for me to

average eighty-eight to ninety mile per hour pitches —
that's why I think I have a good chance of making it to
the majors. It puts me in the top five percent of
pitchers in the entire country for my age. It's also
another reason for me to rest my arm regularly.

Coach calls us into the dugout for one final encouraging word before we take the field.

"Alright, boys. Let's get out there and play our
best. You've got this. Kick Central's ass!" Coach yells.

"Come on, boys," Bomb calls to us. "One, two,
three — "

"Anglers!" we yell in unison, then take our places
and remove our caps for the national anthem. Jonesy
is up first at bat.

"Get 'em."

"Strike him out."

"Jonesy!"

"Kick their butts."

"You got this."

"Let's go!"

Calls and cheers coming from both dugouts and
the crowd mix together. Some cheer on Central, some
encourage Jonesy. Most of the words get lost in the
sea of voices, and it's hard to make out which team
they're cheering for, or maybe I've just learned to tune
it out over the years. Usually, when I'm in game mode,
nothing else catches my attention. Jonesy gets a strike
and two balls before hitting a pitch. The ball sails
toward rightfield as Jonesy races to first.

"Go, go!" we're all yelling as he tries to decipher
the first base coach's movements. The outfielder misses

the catch, and the ball rolls a few feet past him. Jonesy passes first. The outfielder grabs the ball and sends it flying toward second. The second baseman has a foot on the base, leaning out in position to catch the ball. Jonesy slides into second. His foot hits the base seconds before the baseman catches the ball. Yeah!

"Safe!" the umpire announces.

Carter is at bat next. He strikes out in three pitches. *Shit*. Cap's next. His real name is John, but we call him Cap because he always wears a baseball cap, and rarely the same one. He must have a thousand of them. He misses the first pitch but hits the next one. It's a grounder that rolls between the second and third bases and past shortstop. What is Central doing? They never play this badly. Cap rounds first and heads toward second as the ball reaches the left fielder. At the same time, Jonesy rounds third and races toward home. The outfielder hesitates too long, deciding where to throw it. Jonesy gets a run, and Cap reaches third as the third baseman catches the ball. It's a close call.

We all freeze until the ref yells, "Safe!"

Our dugout and fans go nuts. This is the way to play, but it's only the top of first, so we can't afford to get cocky. There's a lot of game left to play.

By the time I take the mound, we're up four runs. Let's hope we can keep doing this. Central has some great hitters, but I'm not worried. I can strike them out.

Looking into the stands, I see Izzy on the top row. She waves, and I tip my baseball cap. Her presence instantly relaxes me. The first hitter steps up to the plate. I take a second to focus, then send a powerful pitch toward home plate. The batter misses. Strike one. Another pitch. Strike two. *Hell, yeah!* Pitch three. Strike three. Easy to hit my stride when I start with an out. Four batters later, they have two outs and guys on first and second. Their next batter comes up to the plate. He's all smug, looking at me like he thinks he's going to get a hit. I wind up and throw a fastball. Strike one. I change it up with a curveball. Strike two.

"Come on, Eli. One more strike," someone calls from the dugout. He swings but misses. Strike three.

By the top of the seventh inning, we're up nine-zero. I'm on the mound with two outs and no one on base. Central's batter steps up. He's already defeated — slumped shoulders, no confidence as he drags the bat to the plate. Two pitches, two strikes. This is it. Once more pitch, one more strike. Deep breath in, let it out as I throw a fastball. He swings and connects. The ball soars over the batter's head and lands behind him. Awesome! Another deep breath, another fastball, another swing, and a miss. Strike three.

My team rushes the mound, patting me on the back and congratulating me. It's our first shutout of the season. It feels damn good.

When I look into the crowd, I see my parents and my sisters cheering. I didn't know Molly and Emma were coming. They don't make many games. Scanning a little further to the right, Captain Mike is sitting with his grandsons. He promised to make every home game this year, and he's kept that promise so far. Sometimes he comes alone, and sometimes he brings the kids. Everyone I care about is here for my biggest game this season. This is the high I crave. It's been a long time since I felt this good.

The celebration continues into the locker room, and word quickly spreads that we're all meeting at Bombs. It's a school night, and we have practice tomorrow afternoon, plus a doubleheader on Saturday. None of us can afford to get caught drinking or being out past curfew. Coach will have us running laps until we die, and our asses will be on the bench.

Hanging out with the team doesn't sound like much fun, but it's important for me to be there. Coach rides me all the time about being a team player and supporting the guys. My friends have become less 'friends' and more 'acquaintances' in the past eleven months. I've distanced myself as much as I can. Their juvenile escapades aren't funny anymore, and I don't give two shits about any of them. My eyes are on the majors, and nothing else matters. Well, nothing except Izzy. She will always matter.

chapter
fourteen

"You comin'?" Cap calls, gaining my attention.

Looking up, I see that the locker room has mostly cleared out. Wow, it didn't take the guys long to shower, change, and bolt. *Okay, pull yourself together and go have some beers with your team.*

"Uh, yeah. I'll be right there."

"You need a ride?" Cap asks.

"Sure, thanks."

Dragging my feet, I follow Cap to his car and toss my gear in the trunk.

"That game was awesome." Cap hands me a beer. He's prepared with a cooler full of beer in the trunk. Nice touch. He grabs one for himself, and we climb into his car. "Damn, boy, you can pitch," he compliments.

"Thanks. It took all of us. Bomb's homerun, your two runs."

"Yeah, but you shutout Central. Fucking *Central!* No one's shut them out in more than ten years."

I can't help but smile. It's unreal. The first pitcher to shut out Central in more than a decade is quite an honor. It might earn me MVP this year.

By the time we park at Bomb's house, our beers are empty. Cap grabs two more from the trunk, and we down them while searching out the keg that usually in the kitchen.

Jonesy sees us coming and meets us halfway with red cups filled to the top.

"Thanks." I don't know how to act around Jonesy.

"Good game," he says.

"Thanks. You, too."

"Loosen up, you two. You both have got to get over yourselves. This little riff is getting old," Cap scolds.

"I'm not the one with the problem," I argue.

"You are the problem," Jonesy retorts with malice.

"Don't start tonight," Cap snaps. "Jonesy, go hang out with Bomb or find a girl. Stay clear of Eli." Cap leans closer to Jonesy. "I'll keep an eye on him."

He *thinks* he whispered it, but I heard him. What does he mean he'll keep an eye on me? Jonesy regards me with concern, then nods to Cap before walking away. I don't know what that exchange was about.

"What the hell was that?" I confront him.

"Nothing. Here, have another beer," he says, handing me the one in his hand. "I'm done drinking. I have to drive."

"Don't tell me 'nothing.' Why did you tell Jonesy you'd keep an eye on me?"

"Because lately, you need a sitter."

"No, I don't."

"Come on, E. Between getting wasted, getting into fights, and being a general asshole to everyone, you need someone to watch you."

"Fuck you! I'm not listening to this bullshit," I bark.

On my way outside, I refill my cup and fill a second one. With a beer in each hand, I walk out to the dock. There are only a few people out here and no one I really know. I walk down the ramp to the gangplank. This is better. The sound of the water lapping against the dock and a distant owl are my only company. I sit against one of the pylons keeping the floating dock in place, drinking my beers and thinking about life.

Sitting out here calms some of my anger. My teammates are conspiring against me. Well, isn't that just perfect? Jonesy and Cap must have had a conversation before the party about babysitting me. I don't need a fucking sitter. I should have gone home and spent time with Izzy. Coming here was stupid.

Anyway, I'm sure Lindsay will be here soon to occupy Cap's time. They've been dating for weeks and seem pretty happy. Unless she's working or Cap's playing ball, they're together.

Much too soon, my cups are empty. I don't want to go back up to the house and face my teammates, but I need a couple more beers.

The party is in full swing. Bomb is on the couch making out with Leah. Well, that's an interesting turn. Stoner is nowhere in sight. Guess she's already moved on. Mitch and Carter are in a heated game of beer pong. Jonesy walks out of one of the bedrooms with a satisfied grin. A girl I've seen around school follows soon after adjusting her dress. I can't remember her name, but I think she's a freshman. Good for you, Jonesy. Others party around the house, and several people are in the pool.

I fill one of my cups and pound it. Then I fill both cups to take them back to the dock. I don't get past the back patio. My head spins, and I stumble a little, then fall into the nearest chair before guzzling both drinks. How many beers have I had?

chapter
fifteen

C oming home drunk out of my mind wasn't my best decision. Apparently, my dad helped me get upstairs. I remember waking up a few times and puking in the trashcan Dad must have left next to my bed. This morning, he woke me up at six so I would have time to clean out the trashcan and clean the bathroom before school. Guess I missed the toilet.

The entire time I clean, I dry heave, but apparently there's nothing left inside me. After the trashcan and bathroom are spic and span, as my mom loves to say, and I've taken a shower, I meet my dad in the kitchen. He made it very clear that we *will* have a talk before I go to school.

The shower didn't do anything to help my hangover, and I've got news for the old man, I won't be making it to school today. My head is pounding, and my stomach is in knots. I'm not in the mood for a lecture from him or Coach or anyone else for that matter. There's no way I can sit through six classes and go to practice. I could barely make it through the shower. I'm not sure how I'm going to sit and listen to Dad's lecture. School is definitely out of the question.

When I get to the kitchen, my dad is sitting at the table drinking his coffee and reading something on his phone.

"Good morning." He's eerily calm. Shit, this can't be good.

"Morning," I mumble, dropping into the chair across from him. "Where's Mom?" I figured they would be double-teaming this lecture. Usually, when I'm in deep shit, they gang up on me.

"She had a breakfast meeting."

Okay, that's odd. My mom doesn't have a job other than helping my dad with the bookkeeping and scheduling at the marina. Whatever. Right now, I don't care where she is or why he's lying about it. My head is too foggy to figure it out, and I can barely keep my eyes open.

He sets his phone and mug on the table and folds his hands together, resting his chin on them.

"Fun night?" he questions.

"Um, I guess."

"Well, good. Glad you think getting piss-ass drunk and having to be carried home by three of your friends is a good time."

Three? What is he talking about? Cap brought me home. He must see the confusion in my eyes.

"Don't remember much, do you?"

"I remember," I snap.

"Oh, that's good. Who brought you home?"

"Cap."

I answer too quickly. I should have thought about it more. Tried to remember. It wouldn't have done any good. I have no idea what happened last night. I don't remember much between drinking a few beers and puking my guts out.

"Cap drove," he confirms.

"Why are you being this way? I don't fucking remember! Just say whatever it is you're going to say!"

"Watch your language and your tone, young man. This is your doing, so don't take your anger out on me."

"Sorry," I mumble. I'm not sorry, but it's what he wants to hear, so I indulge him.

"Cap drove you home, but it took Cap, Jonesy, and Sam to get you in the house. I had to help them get you upstairs. You were fighting us the whole way. You're strong. I'll give you that. I'm surprised no one ended up with a black eye. You weren't making it easy on any of us."

He's lying. There's no way I was drunk enough to act that way. I'm usually a subdued drunk. Drink a few beers, walk home, and sleep it off in the treehouse. Calm, quiet, and no one gets hurt. He has to be lying. I bet this is some 'scared straight' shit he's trying to pull. 'Let's scare Eli. Lie to him so he won't drink anymore.' Yeah, well... Jokes on you. Not gonna quit having a good time just because I took it too far one night.

"That's it, son? You don't have anything to say for yourself?"

"You're lying." *Shut up, Eli. Why did you say that out loud? Come on, brain—function.*

"You want to try that again?"

"No. I'm tired, and my head hurts," I bark, getting up too fast and knocking my chair over. All I need is another broken chair. The noise sends shockwaves through my head, and that pain rolls my stomach. There can't possibly be anything left for me to puke up. "I'm going back to bed."

"The hell you are!" my dad bellows. "You're going to pick up that chair, get your bag, and get your ass to school."

"That's not happening," I clap back.

Not waiting for him to respond, I head for my room as fast as my legs will carry me. They aren't working much better than the rest of my body. Everything feels heavy. My muscles ache, my head pounds, and my stomach hurts. This sucks. I've never had a hangover like this. Fuck, maybe I'm, still drunk.

My bed has never looked so inviting. I pull the covers over my head to block out the brightening sun and pull the extra pillow close, wrapping my arms around it. Ever since I can remember, I've always slept with two pillows. One under my head and one held in my arms. It's weird, and I'd never live it down if the guys found out, but it's comforting. I never had a favorite blanket or stuffed animal when I was little, but I've always needed two pillows. Snuggling up to my pillow, I get as comfortable as I can with this pounding headache and try to fall asleep. I should have taken some aspirin before I laid down.

About the time I get relaxed, my door swings open. It was worth a shot.

"Get up!" my dad yells, yanking the covers off me.

"Go away!" I bark back. My eyes are still closed as my left hand searches for the comforter, but it comes up empty.

"Get up!" my dad bellows again.

This time he grabs my arm and pulls me out of the bed. My knees hit the floor before Dad lifts me to my feet. Nausea hits me, and I run to the bathroom. After several minutes of dry heaving, I fall back against the tub as my dad stands in the doorway, staring me down.

"Done?" he asks.

"I think so."

He offers me a hand. I accept it, and he pulls me to my feet. I stumble back into my room and find my comforter on the floor. As I climb back into bed, my dad grabs my arm.

"Nope," he says, turning me toward him. "You made this choice, and you're going to live with the consequences. Put on some clothes and get downstairs. I'll drive you to school."

The look on his face tells me not to argue.

I drop my shoulders. "Give me five minutes," I relent.

He nods once and leaves me to get myself together. Aspirin is a must. Searching the cabinet in my bathroom, I come up empty-handed. Instead, I brush my teeth and pull on some jeans and a clean t-shirt. Then I grab my backpack before seeking out my dad. I find him in the kitchen sipping another cup of coffee. This time it's in the travel mug he takes to work every day.

"Here." He hands me a glass of water and two aspirin. I toss the pills in my mouth and drink the whole glass of water. I didn't realize how much I needed it until I started drinking. "Take this. It will help your stomach."

I look in the paper bag and find a sleeve of Ritz crackers, a bottle of Gatorade, a bottle of water, and some Pepto. Nice. This might not save the day, but it will make it a little more bearable.

"Thanks."

As soon as he pulls out of the driveway, he starts in on me again. "What were you thinking? You could have gotten alcohol poisoning or worse."

"I didn't drink that much."

"You couldn't walk on your own."

"What do you want me to say? I pitched a shutout against Central. They're the best team in the state. That deserved a celebration."

"I agree. You pitched a damn good game and should have celebrated. Drinking to the point you can't handle yourself is more than a celebration. You're going down the wrong path, Eli. You barely see your friends outside of school, none of them come to the house anymore. Your grades are crap. You're passing just enough to stay on the team and teetering on a thin line. You're angry, and the mood swings are giving *all* of us whiplash. I want to know what's gotten into you lately. What's wrong with you? Did some-thing happen that you need to talk about?"

Did something happen? Is he *serious*? My life is in a downward spiral. Everything went to shit almost a year ago, and it isn't getting better. How can everyone act like nothing happened? How can he not remember? Am I crazy? Is there something wrong with me? Should I be over it by now?

When I don't respond, he sighs and continues, much calmer this time. "Look, Eli. I know you've had a tough time this past year. What you went through last spring was hell, but it's time to find a way to work past it. Hurting yourself and your friends isn't the answer.

"Nothing's wrong," I lie.

He'll never understand what I'm going through. No one knows how hard these past few months have been for me. There's no point in telling anyone, they won't care. My friends don't even remember.

"So, you just got drunk for fun?" he asks, getting angry again.

"Sure, Dad," I bite out sarcastically.

"If you aren't willing to talk to me about whatever is going on with you, then you need some time to think about your actions and shitty choices you've been making. You're grounded for the next six weeks. School, baseball, home. That's it. No friends. No parties. *No treehouse.* You can have your phone when you're at school or practice, but you need to leave it in the kitchen when you get home. You can spend all that extra time studying for a change. Maybe you will finally bring your grades up."

"I doubt that."

This isn't fair. I don't deserve to be grounded for six weeks, but it's not worth the argument. I don't care about any parts of the punishment except the treehouse. He can't keep me from going up there. He can't keep me away from Izzy for that long. It isn't right.

Dad pulls up in front of the school at five after eight. Ten minutes to get to homeroom. I'll make it in plenty of time, but it also means time to run into Cap, Sam, and Jonesy. I'm not ready to face them or the rest of the team after last night. I feel like shit and have no desire to fake remorse this early.

Homeroom is uneventful. I managed to make it this far without talking to anyone. As soon as the bell rings signaling the end of homeroom, I beeline it for the door.

"Sterling," Coach stops me as I reach the doorway. "I need to talk to you."

Crap. I step aside and wait for the room to empty, then I close the door, but make no effort to walk any further into the room.

"You played great yesterday." His words relax me. Maybe I'm not in trouble. He motions for me to sit at the desk closest to his own. Reluctantly, I oblige. "There was a scout at the game, and he liked what they saw."

"Okay..." What's he getting at? I'm too young for them to take much notice. Scouts are looking at juniors and seniors. They're trying to lock in the seniors they've been talking to for a year. Signing day will be here soon and they're starting to look at the juniors to decide who's worth their attention next year. I don't matter until right now.

"You're a great pitcher, Sterling, but I don't think you realize how good you are all around. Not a lot of pitchers can hit home runs. A home run *with* men on second and third. *That* gets people's attention."

"What are you getting at, Coach?" I ask.

"There was a scout here from Boden Academy. He wants me to set up a meeting with you and your parents."

"Boden? Are you serious?"

Boden Academy is outside of Fort Lauderdale, over five hours from here and on the other side of the state. It's a boarding school known for sending some of the best players of all time to the majors. You're practically guaranteed a spot on a minor league team if you play baseball for Boden. The great players go straight from Boden to the majors, and the crappy players get recruited by Division 1 schools.

"The recruiter is in town through the weekend. He wants to watch you play again tomorrow. Let your parents know that he'd like to have dinner with all of us tomorrow night. Seven o'clock at Poseidon."

Poseidon. Fancy. It's the best seafood restaurant in town, and that's saying a lot. Living on the Gulf, almost every restaurant serves good seafood.

"Um, yeah, sure. I'll text them and let you know. Thanks, Coach."

"Good job, Sterling." Coach hands me a late pass as the second bell rings.

"Thanks," I say, waving the pass at him.

As soon as I step into the hallway, I text my dad.

> Me: Can we have dinner tomorrow
> night with Coach and a recruiter from
> Boden Academy? He wants to talk to
> me. And you guys.

I hit send as I walk to math. Mrs. Thatcher is a witch about phones, so I silence mine and put in my backpack. I'll have to check it after class. She gives me a dirty look when I hand her the late pass. She doesn't say anything, but I know she hates it when athletes get special treatment. It's a legit late pass, it's not like I was screwing off.

"Take your seat, Mr. Sterling." Always formal, Mrs. Thatcher never uses our first names. It's Mr. or Miss and our last names. Weird.

chapter
sixteen

Dad called during lunch and voiced his concerns about meeting the recruiter because of my behavior. He wouldn't give me a straight answer but agreed to have a conversation about Boden tonight.

"In the kitchen," Mom calls as I close the front door.

Great. I roll my eyes. That means she wants me to join her. I'm exhausted, and my head is still pounding. School and practice were awful, lunch didn't stay down, and I spent more time at practice dry heaving than actually practicing. For once, Coach went easy on me. He left me alone during practice and told me to go shower while the team ran a few laps. Does he know I got drunk last night? It isn't like Coach to give any of us a break when he sees us struggling, especially if it's because we did something stupid. It doesn't matter why he was nice to me—I'm grateful.

"Have a seat. I'll get you something to eat."

"I'm not hungry," I answer.

She hands me a bottle of Gatorade and busies herself at the counter for about five minutes before placing a plate with a slice of dry toast and some mashed potatoes on it in front of me.

"Try to eat something," she encourages. When I look up to argue, her eyes are full of concern. My chest tightens with guilt at the sight. I quickly look away. She's worried about me, likely because of my behavior and not because I haven't eaten. As I push the plate away, my stomach growls, giving away how hungry I am. Mom rubs a consoling hand through my hair.

"Have you eaten anything today?" she asks quietly.

"Some crackers Dad gave me and a little lunch."

"Did you keep it down?"

"No," I admit.

"How was practice?"

"A bitch."

"Language."

Why are my parents so hung up on me cussing? All my friends do it. They're just words. It's not like my parents don't use the same ones. Okay, my dad, not Mom.

Mom walks to the stove, stirs something, and then sits across from me at the table.

"Where's Dad?" It's after seven, and he's nowhere in sight.

"Lola Anne had trouble during the charter today. Everyone's fine, but she started taking on water, and the passengers had to be rescued by the Coast

Guard. Dad's still at the marina handling everything."

Lola Anne is Captain Joe's boat. It passed inspection last month.

"What happened?" Dad's boats are always in great condition. He inspects them every month and requires the captains to do inspections at least once a week. He prides himself on the safety of his employees and clients.

"I'm not sure. They're trying to figure that out tonight."

"I'm glad everyone is safe."

"Me, too."

Mom watches me in silence as I try to force down the toast. I know I need to get something on my stomach, but my insides are protesting every bite.

"Tell me what happened last night."

Here we go. "Nothing happened. I had a couple of beers."

"You couldn't walk."

"You saw me?" I'm shocked she was awake that late.

"Cap called to tell us they were bringing you home and needed help. Your dad and I both got dressed. From the way Cap described it, we thought we were going to have to take you to the hospital. I sat with you all night to make sure you were safe. Your dad offered, but he needed to sleep so he could work today, so I stayed up all night and watched you." She chokes back a few tears as she recounts everything.

Guilt tightens my chest. I didn't mean to upset my mom.

"Oh, I didn't know. Dad said you were at a breakfast meeting."

"I asked him not to tell you. When he came in to wake you up, I went to bed. It took me most of the afternoon to decide whether or not to share this with you, but you need to understand how bad off you were last night. What you did was extremely dangerous."

"I'm sorry. I didn't mean to scare you."

"It's about more than me being worried last night. You're spiraling. You're out of control. You need help, and you won't talk to your dad or me."

"I'm not out of control. I got drunk. Once."

"More than once. What about all those nights you sleep in the treehouse after a party at Bomb's?"

"Wh-what?" How the hell does she know that?

"I know you, Eli. The past year has been tough on you. You aren't dealing with everything that happened in the right way."

"I'm fine. There's no secret meaning behind my drinking last night. I had an incredible game and drank one too many. There's no underlying problem." The lie flows easily.

"So, you're sticking to that story?"

"What story?"

"You simply got drunk for the sake of getting drunk."

"Yes."

"Then we have a different issue. You're sixteen. You aren't old enough to drink, much less get drunk.

I'm disappointed in the choices you've been making these past months, but last night, you went overboard. I keep thinking you will turn things around, but your choices are getting worse. I sat with you last night because I love you and want you to be safe, but I can barely look at you today. I'm so damn angry at you, Eli. I think your father is being lenient by only grounding you for six weeks."

That might be the first time I've ever heard my mother cuss. Hearing how she feels about me is like a knife to my heart. No, stabbing me wouldn't hurt this much. Blinking back a few tears, I focus on moving the potatoes around my plate. She doesn't need to see me upset. I don't want her to know her words got to me.

Steeling myself, I look her in the eye after a few moments. "I'm not a drunk. Sorry you think I'm such a screw-up and ruined your perfect family. Guess you should have stopped after two. It's not like you wanted more kids." The hateful words pour out of my mouth. My brain tells me to stop, but my mouth doesn't listen. "I was an accident that never should have happened. All I've ever done is fuck up. That isn't going to change, so you should have gotten rid of me when you had the chance."

"Eli!" my mother cries. "What are you talking about? We love you very much and wanted you. Yes, we were surprised when I got pregnant, but being surprised is *very different* than being disappointed. Your father and I were excited when we got the news, and nothing will ever change that." She tries to say pretty words, but I hear the sadness as her voice cracks. My words crushed her. I knew they would, but I said them anyway. Nothing I said to her was true, but my anger won't allow me to apologize.

While I play with the potatoes, my mother goes to the stove and turns off the burner where she was cooking a pot of soup. She starts loading the dishwasher and cleaning the kitchen. What do I say? It's no secret that I wasn't planned, but I know my parents love me. They've always called me the 'best surprise.' They have never made me feel unwanted, so why did I say that to her?

Slowly, I gather the strength to leave the table. I dump the uneaten mashed potatoes in the trash and place my plate and fork in the dishwasher. My mom looks at me expectantly, but I turn my back on her and go to my room. Seconds after I shut my door, she knocks and then opens it without waiting for me to respond.

"We aren't finished. Your father told me about Boden."

"Okay." My shoes land with a thud as I kick them off.

"I'm not sure it's a good idea."

"Yeah, Dad said that." My shirt comes off next. I need to go to bed. My body is completely worn out, and we have two games tomorrow.

"You've made too many questionable decisions lately. Being unsupervised that far away concerns us."

"I won't be unsupervised. They have adults watching the students."

"It's more freedom than you can handle."

"I can handle it," I argue, tossing my jeans on the floor and laying back against my pillow. Mom doesn't seem to be getting the message that I don't want to talk. I want to go to bed.

"We aren't sure it's the best option for you right now, but—"

But. There's a but. I sit up, hoping for good news.

"We think it's worth speaking to Coach about the dinner. I'm not saying we'll agree to meet the recruiter, but your dad will call Coach and talk about Boden. Then we'll decide if we're going to dinner."

"Okay," I agree. It wasn't what I wanted to hear, but a call to Coach is better than an outright no. "Thank you."

"Get some rest." Mom pulls the covers over me and runs her hand through my hair. "You truly were our best surprise, and no matter what, I will *always* love you." She kisses my forehead and then walks to the door.

Mom is almost out of my room when I get up the courage to speak. "I'm sorry." Two words are all I can manage right down. Mom smiles, then closes my door.

I've done an extraordinary job of disappointing my parents in the past eleven months. Good thing they have my perfect sisters to balance life out. Sleep will be good for me. Hearing what a disappointment I am from my parents isn't how I wanted to start, or end, this day.

Truthfully, I'm not even sure Boden is something I want. Leaving my friends, family, and everything I know in high school never crossed my mind. Whether I'm actually offered the opportunity is up in the air. Suppose I am given a chance to play for Boden—in that case, it may not be financially feasible, or my parents could flat out say no because of my behavior, grades, attitude, or any number of things, really.

None of these what-ifs matter right now. First, my parents have to agree to the dinner. Then we'll see what the recruiter has to say. In my opinion, a meeting is worth our time. I said all of this and more to my dad when he called me during lunch. At least Dad is going to call Coach and discuss it further with him. That's a start.

chapter
seventeen

This day flew by and no there is barely enough time for me to get dressed before we had to leave for dinner. My mind relives the entire day, while I get dressed and brush my teeth.

I don't know what Coach said, but it worked. My parents told me at breakfast that they would come to dinner tonight. Even though I was exhausted and still hungover, I barely slept, but I feel better this morning. My dad came home around ten, and I thought about getting up to ask if he talked to Coach, but I was too miserable to do anything but stay in bed last night.

Dad didn't have much to say to me this morning, which was fine. I don't have anything to say to him. This whole grounding thing pisses me off, but I guess Dad is doing his parental duty. I screwed up, and whether I agree with his punishment or not, I have to face the consequences. Yeah, I'm not telling him that.

Mom was nice to me and made a huge breakfast like she does every Saturday. She tried to talk to me a little, but I could still hear the sadness in her voice. The things I said to her last night must have really hurt her. She wasn't her usual, bubbly self.

With this Boden thing on the table now, I need to be more careful about sneaking out and drinking. If there is any chance of me getting into the school, I have to change my behavior. Getting in more trouble will put a stop to everything.

I'm still not back to a hundred percent after getting so wasted Thursday night. It shouldn't take this long to get through a hangover. Maybe I did overdo it. Feeling like crap wasn't good for my game. I didn't play my best, and knowing the recruiter from Boden was in the stands was nerve-wracking. It made everything a little more real. Every play was more important than in any other game I've played. Every error hit me like a ton of bricks. During the first game, I struck out my first time at bat. Then I got tagged out my second time hitting. I missed a catch while playing outfielder, allowing the other team to get two runs. We won that game, but not because I helped the team. The second game was much better. The butterflies had calmed themselves, and I was more focused. I got two base hits and a homerun. When I was in the outfield, I caught three balls for outs. Winning the second game boosted my confidence a little since I feel like I actually contributed.

It was almost four by the time I made it home and showered. I tried working on a paper for history that's due on Tuesday, but I fell asleep and didn't wake up until after six.

As soon as I'm ready, I rush downstairs where my parents are waiting.

"Ready?" Mom asks with an encouraging smile, picking up her purse from the hook near the front door.

"Yep." I hope I'm ready.

My stomach is doing backflips as Dad pulls into a space in Poseidon's parking lot. Why am I so nervous? Going to Boden would help me get to the majors, but plenty of great players get there without some fancy high school, playing D1 in college, or starting in the minors. I need to believe I'm good enough *without* Boden. That's been a challenge recently. This season hasn't gone the way I'd hoped. Being benched so much at the beginning wasn't good. It screwed a little with my stats but being a utility player gave me the chance to gain stats in areas other than pitching. I'm only allowed to pitch in a certain number of games anyway. Honestly, it messed with my head, too. I haven't played my best in some games, and it's screwing with my confidence. The game against Central was the first time I truly felt great about a game this season. That's never happened before. Usually, I'm confident in every game I play. Some people might even call me cocky.

I knew this year would be different. After the way last season ended, I wasn't sure I should play this year. Honestly, I considered quitting for good. My dad wasn't happy when I decided not to play summer ball for the first time since I was eleven. When I told him in August that I didn't want to play fall ball, he hit the roof, gave me a speech about responsibility and how he let the summer ball decision go, but I wasn't going to throw my entire future away by sitting on my ass for another three months. He couldn't understand that I needed a break. Since I was old enough to walk, I've been playing sports. When I turned eleven, the middle school let me play on the baseball team, even though I was still in fifth grade, and when I turned twelve, I started playing year-round. By last summer, I was burned out.

"You ready for this?" Dad asks, patting me on the shoulder.

It's been a long time since I've seen Dad excited or proud when it comes to me. Tonight, I can see it in his eyes. He isn't one to dole out compliments easily, but it's not hard to know exactly how he feels by looking in his eyes. He doesn't have a poker face and rarely needs to tell you how he feels. Although, he hasn't had much trouble telling me his thoughts about my 'shitty choices' and 'deplorable behavior' lately—his words, not mine. Fun times being a disappointment to my parents. I should be used to it by now. Unless it's baseball, they don't have much use for me. *That's not true, and you know it.* I'm tired of them being on my case, but I know they love me. Lately, I've had a hard time remembering that and if I said any of this out loud, it would sound like my parents are mean and unsupportive, which isn't true. Dad is proud of me right now, and that's where my head needs to be.

This past year has been hard. The weight of it all is slowly suffocating me. My parents don't understand, so I keep it all inside. I tried talking to Jonesy a few months ago, but he told me to stop being so drama queen and get over it. It's not that easy. One choice last April changed my entire existence, and no one understands.

"Ready," I respond, taking a deep breath and letting it out slowly. Maybe this is what I need to get back on track, or maybe it will completely derail me and send my life careening out of control.

chapter
eighteen

The sounds and smells of Poseidon hit me as soon as I walk inside. I hold the door open for my parents. The place is packed, and conversations blend together from every direction. The huge fountain in the center with a statue of Poseidon mixes the rush of water with the cacophony of voices. From the left, piano music floats out of the bar. The aroma of gourmet meals hits me as we are led to our table. The smoky scent of grilled steaks, the faint smell of seafood, and the strong aromas of garlic and lemon fill the air.

Coach Karson and Mr. Barnes, the recruiter, are already seated. Introductions are made as we join them. My nerves are in overdrive as I fidget with the bottom of my tie. My parents went a little overboard by insisting that I wear a coat and tie. Sweat drips down my back, and I can't get comfortable. My Dad lightly knocks my knee with his—a silent warning to be still. *You can do this, Eli. You've never had trouble talking to people. Relax and turn on the charm.* My silent pep talk doesn't help much, but I sit up a little straighter and square my shoulders. *Be a man. You can do this.*

"Good evening. Welcome to Poseidon. I'm Carrie, and I'll be taking care of you this evening. Can I get anyone a drink from the bar?"

"Sauvignon Blanc," my mom orders.

"Would you like the house Sauvignon Blanc? It's on the happy hour menu for four dollars."

"That will be great, thank you."

"Ashton IPA." My dad orders a beer from the local brewery that opened a couple of years ago.

"That sounds good. I'll have the Ashton IPA as well," Mr. Barnes adds.

"Just water for me," Coach says.

I've never seen him drink alcohol. Not that I have many meals with Coach, but usually when we travel, the other coaches and parents have a drink with dinner, but never Coach.

"Sweet tea," I order when she looks at me.

I don't really like soda. It's probably been four or five years since I drank one. I tend to drink water or sports drinks unless I'm at a party, but I do love a glass of sweet tea.

"Excellent! Can I start you with some appetizers?"

"No, thank you," comes from everyone at the table.

"I'll be right back with those drinks."

Carrie bounces away and the heat is back on me. Now, it's conversation time. My first real conversation with a recruiter. What if I say something stupid? Hell, he might not be interested anymore after my performance today.

"Eli," Mr. Barnes calls from across the table. My stomach bottoms out. What is wrong with me? *Pull yourself together.* "Tell me a little about yourself."

What? How do I answer that question? Does he want to know about baseball, school, or personal stuff? It's a stupid question.

"U-um, W-well," I stutter. "I love baseball. I think I'm a pretty good outfielder —"

"No," he stops me. "Tell me about Eli. I know what you can do on the baseball field. I want to know who you are off the field."

Well, shit. Who am I off the field? Carrie returns with our drinks, giving me a chance to think about what I want to say.

If you ask my parents, I'm a drunk and terrible son. There was a time when I liked hanging out with my friends. I spend an unhealthy amount of time in a kid's treehouse with my best friend. None of that is what he wants to hear.

"Are you ready to order?" she asks.

"I think so," Coach replies.

We take turns placing our orders, and Carrie is gone too soon. I needed more time to figure out my answer.

"So, Eli, you were getting ready to tell me about yourself," Mr. Barnes reminds me.

"Oh, okay." I adjust in my seat, giving myself a few more seconds. "Baseball is a huge part of who I am and who I want to be, but my friends are important to me, too. I enjoy hanging out with them." That's not entirely true, but he probably doesn't want to know that Izzy is the only person who truly matters to me. "I'm loyal and work hard for what I want. I do alright in school. I love my family. I enjoy fishing and working at the marina my dad owns." They aren't all lies. Somewhere among the bullshit is a little bit of truth.

"Coach Karson said similar things about you. You're an impressive young man."

"Thank you." Guess he doesn't know that my grades stink, and I've gotten in a couple of fights lately. He probably wouldn't find me impressive then.

"I like what I saw on the field this week." He must see the shock in my eyes because he chuckles a little before continuing. "Thursday, I planned to watch the game and talk to your coach about you. After I saw you pitch a shutout against the top team in the state, I wanted to see more, so I extended my trip through the weekend. You did *not* disappoint. You had to work through some nerves in game one, but that's not unusual the first time you know you're being scouted. You turned that around in game two. That's what good players do. Lesser players let the nerves settle in and can't move past them."

Wow. I've never looked at it that way. "Thank you, sir. The baseball field always feels like home. It's where I belong."

"I can see that. So does your coach."

Our food arrives, interrupting the conversation again.

"This looks amazing. Florida sure does have the best seafood!" Mr. Barnes exclaims. "I grew up in the mid-west. Not much seafood there. When I moved to Florida ten years ago, I had shrimp and lobster for the first time," he admits.

"Seriously? I can't imagine living anywhere without great seafood," I tell him.

"I don't know. I lived almost thirty years without it, but I guess I didn't know what I was missing."

Mr. Barnes digs into his lobster pasta, halting the conversation. The rest of us join him. We haven't eaten here since Molly graduated last May, and we came to celebrate. We always have an abundance of fish in the freezer. Sometimes, Dad brings home fresh-caught seafood from the marina, so there's usually no need to waste money at a restaurant. But it is nice to have a meal out once in a while.

The surf and turf is my favorite meal here. You get to choose from filet mignon, ribeye, or New York strip for the turf portion, and salmon, sheepshead, ahi tuna, or lobster tail for the surf portion. It also comes with two sides. As always, I ordered a ribeye—medium rare—and sheepshead with asparagus and garlic mashed potatoes. It's the best meal on the menu in my opinion. We fall into easy conversation about the weather, fishing, and the upcoming MLB season. It's a lot more fun when I'm not the focus. Much too soon, we finish our meals, and Carrie clears our plates.

"Can I offer anyone dessert or coffee?" she questions.

While the adults order coffee, I ask for a slice of

key lime pie, and my dad orders the peanut butter chocolate cheesecake, but I know my mom will eat most of it. Coach declines and Mr. Barnes orders a slice of carrot cake. Okay, but do carrots really belong in a dessert? I hear it's delicious, but I was not a fan the one time I tried it.

"That was one of the best meals I have had while traveling," Mr. Barnes admits. "Great suggestion, Bill," he says to Coach. He pauses briefly, then turns to my parents. "Eli is a remarkable player. He has a great future ahead of him. After the games today, I spoke to our headmaster and coaching staff. I sent them some videos I took, and we all agree that Boden would be honored to have Eli on our team. Our star pitcher is graduating, and we'd like to offer Eli a scholarship for the next two years. He would be one of our starting pitchers."

A scholarship? Starting pitcher? This is a bigger deal than I realized. There are twelve guys playing in the majors right now who all graduated from Boden and went straight there. That doesn't include all the players who went to the minors or college first, or those who have already retired from the game. Close to a thousand Boden graduates have played some portion of their career in the majors since the school opened in 1935. Many are hailed as some of the greatest players in history.

Now, the hard part—getting my parents on board and figuring out if this is truly what I want. It's an amazing offer but is it right for me? Is this my next step? I don't even know how Mr. Barnes found me. Well, I guess that's his job.

"Thank you, Mr. Barnes. We're very proud of Eli and his accomplishments on the baseball field." Way to avoid being proud of me in general, Dad. "While we understand this is a huge opportunity for Eli, I'm not sure he's ready for the responsibility that comes with living away from home." What the hell? "My wife and I need some time to think this over."

"I understand. I don't want an answer today. Eli, you have a lot to consider, and I want you to have some honest conversations with your parents. This is a big decision for all of you."

"Yes, sir." At least one adult recognizes that I get a say.

Mr. Barnes insists on picking up the check, probably another attempt to get on my parents' good side. Then he and Coach walk us to our truck.

"It was nice meeting you, Eli," Mr. Barnes says, offering me his hand. I shake it.

"It was nice to meet you, too, sir."

"Mr. and Mrs. Sterling, wonderful to meet you both. Take the time you need to explore Eli's options."

"Nice to meet you as well," my mom says.

"We will consider everything you are offering and let you know our decision," Dad adds, shaking Mr. Barnes' hand.

"Have a good night. See you at practice tomorrow." Coach waves, and I wave back.

The drive home is quiet. My parents sit in silence

in the front as I scroll through my phone in the back. Bomb is having another party to celebrate our latest wins. Everyone's there, except me. I open an app and scroll through the pictures everyone's been posting. Looks like I'm missing one hell of a party.

"Mr. Barnes seems nice. It was good of him to come all this way to meet you," Mom comments from the front seat.

Way to completely avoid the subject. He made me an incredible offer. This is the biggest decision of my life, and they're acting like it's nothing. That tells me all I need to know. They've already decided, and the answer is no. My opinion isn't going to matter. It never does. I'm not sure I want to accept the offer, but I want my opinion heard. I deserve that much.

"Yeah, he was nice," I clip.

If they were going to have a discussion with me tonight, Dad would have said something as soon as we got in the car. He's going to let this sit. Probably another way to punish me.

Pulling into the driveway, I decide to go for it. I know better, but I can't help myself. "He's offering me a great opportunity."

"One that we are not discussing tonight."

Shot down. My parents get out of the car and walk toward the house. What the hell? By the time I climb out of the back and get to the door, my parents are inside. Mom is halfway up the stairs, and Dad is opening a beer in the kitchen.

"Dad..."

"No, son. Your mother and I will talk about it later then get back to you with our decision."

"Shouldn't I get to help make the decision? It affects my life."

"You're sixteen and have proven to us over and over that you are not capable of making mature choices."

I follow my dad into the living room. He plops down on the old, brown couch and picks up the remote, an indication that he's done talking.

"Is this because I got drunk once?"

"Once? Do you honestly believe I don't know about the times you come home drunk and sleep it off in the treehouse? Do you think you're being quiet when you try to sneak back in after we've gone to bed?"

Shit. I thought I *was* being quiet. Mom brought this up yesterday, but I figured she was baiting me to see if I'd out myself. Usually, I have a few drinks and walk home too drunk to drive but sober enough to take care of myself. Thursday was an anomaly. My friends don't normally have to carry me home.

"Partying with my friends doesn't mean I can't make this decision, or at the very least have an opinion about it."

"It's late, and I'm tired. We are not discussing this further. Your mother and I will discuss it later. Go to bed."

"This is bullshit!" I yell before rushing out of the room and upstairs.

I slam my bedroom door behind me. I know I'm acting like a child, which isn't helping my argument about being able to make a mature decision. In fact, it's doing the opposite and satisfying my father, proving to him that I'm immature and childish.

chapter
nineteen

I t's been three days, and my parents haven't mentioned the offer from Boden. Coach asked me today which way we're leaning. I didn't know what to say. Their silence is likely a no, but I don't want Coach to know they haven't talked to me about it yet. He seemed uncomfortable when he brought it up. He's probably torn between wanting to support me if I go to Boden and not wanting to lose his best pitcher. It's a tough spot; I don't envy his position. Mine isn't any better. I don't want to lie to Coach, but I don't have any information to share. I kept the discussion as vague as possible and bolted from the locker room as soon as practice ended.

"Yo, E!" Cap calls, catching up to me in the parking lot after practice. "Some of us are heading down to Barnacles to grab some food. Wanna come?"

I think about it for a few seconds. I want to spend time with my friends, but I'll be in more trouble if I'm late getting home. It would be fun to hang out and relax for a while. It would take my mind off Boden. Ashton Marina is at the north end of the docks, so it's doubtful that my dad will come to the restaurant and catch me, but there's a chance.

"Nah. I'm still grounded."

"Oh, yeah. I forgot."

The look of pity in his eyes annoys me. I don't need his pity. I got caught—now I'm paying for it.

"Next time," I promise. Yeah, next time in about five weeks. My sentence just started.

Not giving him a chance to take any more pity on me, I turn and walk toward Marlin Street.

"Wait up, Eli," Jonesy calls from behind me. What does he want?

"Aren't you going with the guys?"

"I can catch up with them later. Let's walk."

Jonesy takes a few steps, but when I don't move, he pauses and motions for me to follow him. Okay, this is weird. Reluctantly, I fall in step beside him. This is awkward and seriously uncomfortable. We haven't exactly been friends lately. I don't know what to say to him.

"What do you want, Jonesy?" I snap.

"I know you've been struggling this past year, but you have to stop taking it out on everyone else."

"Not this shit again," I groan.

"Listen to me," Jonesy barks.

"I'm not listening to your bullshit today."

"Look, Eli. I get it."

"No, you don't fucking get it. No one gets it."

"I'm trying—"

"Trying? What exactly are you 'trying?'"

"To be your friend. To help you."

"I don't need your help. Remember? I'm just a drama queen."

Jonesy steps in front of me and stops. Crossing my arms, I look him in the eye. "What?"

"I'm sorry I said that to you. It was wrong and mean." He pauses briefly like he's carefully considering his next words. "What happened really fucked you up, didn't it?" When I don't respond, he continues. "I should have been a better friend and realized that you weren't just being an asshole. You're still hurting, and you're not over it."

"I'm fine."

"You are so *far* from fine. You're fucked in the head, man."

"Fuck you, Jonesy. You don't know anything about me or the kind of hell this past year has been."

"Because you shut me out. I was your best friend and then nothing. Last year, you were the first one to want to hang out. This year, you don't want to have anything to do with us." Jonesy takes a deep breath and runs his hands through his hair. "Okay, you're right. I don't understand what you've been going through. I can't imagine how messed up you are over that shit, but I'm still your friend, and I want to help you. I'm here for you. Whatever you need."

"Too little, too late. Leave me alone!" I bark before turning down my street.

Jonesy doesn't follow me. I don't look back to see

if he waits for me to turn around or walks away to go meet the guys.

The sun is quickly sinking in front of me as I reach my house. We only live about a mile from the school at the end of Gulf Way, but it was the longest walk of my life this afternoon. Jonesy had no right to follow me home and pretend he wanted to help. I don't need anyone. He can fuck right off.

Gulf Way is a short street with only eight houses that dead ends near the water. Three houses sit on either side. At the end, our house and Izzy's stand side by side facing the others. The sand oak with our tree-house rests on the property line. The water on this end of Ashton Bay is calm. It's the sound that connects the Gulf to the river that separates Ashton Bay from the mainland. The island is only a mile and a half at this end and we can see the marina and the Gulf. As you travel south, the island gets larger, and at its widest point, it's almost six miles across. From north to south, Ashton Bay is about twelve miles. The year-round population is close to ten thousand. Small enough that people know who I am—partly because of baseball and partly because of my dad. Baseball and fishing are Ashton Bay's two claims to fame, and Dad owns the largest of the three marinas on the island. The other two can only handle about fifteen boats each at any given time. Depending on the size, Ashton Marina can handle between a hundred and a hundred and twenty-five boats, plus the five charter fishing boats he owns.

Sometimes, it stinks living where everyone knows

me. I've never been able to get away with anything—it always gets back to my family. Being the local baseball star isn't all bad, though. It gets me special treatment at a lot of places. Many of the locally owned businesses sponsor the baseball team, so I get free, or discounted stuff at their establishments.

My dad doesn't need to know the truth, but I like working on the docks. Cleaning the boats, going out on charters, and fishing is fun. I love working with Captain Mike. We get along well, and sometimes, he lets me drive the boat when we go out. I've learned a lot from him over the years. He's easy to talk to and treats me like an equal. It's better than working with my dad. He's always on my case about something, driving me insane. The older I get, the less we get along.

When I was a kid, we did everything together. My dad taught me how to fish and about working on the docks. We built the treehouse with Izzy and her dad. He taught me how to play baseball. We had some great times together. It was the boys against the girls. Mom did stuff with Molly and Emma that they enjoyed, and my dad and I did things I liked. Once my sisters moved out, and I became a teenager, things shifted. Now, it's my parents against me. It gets lonely sometimes.

When I arrive home, my parents have already eaten dinner. I don't see my mom, so she must be upstairs already with her wine and book. It's early, but maybe she's extra tired tonight. Dad is on the couch watching a basketball game. The MLB season starts next week, so that's all we'll watch for the next few months. I hope the Marlins have a decent season this year. They haven't won the World Series in a long time, but they're my favorite team and I'll stick by them. Of course, I won't get to pick and choose my team when I get to the majors. The team I play for will be determined by who drafts me. It would be cool to play for the Marlins, though.

In the oven, I come up empty-handed. No dinner. I open the refrigerator and find a bowl waiting for me — seared ahi tuna salad with a ginger dressing. Nice. I grab a fork and a glass of water then join my dad on the couch. We watch the game in silence while I eat. It's a little awkward, but maybe I'm being paranoid.

"How was practice?" he finally speaks.

"Brutal. Coach worked us hard, but we've got a tough schedule the next two weeks then that big tournament, so we need to put in the work."

It's the truth. Practice kicked my ass today, but the next few weeks are going to be rough. After the tournament in Tampa, we'll have it easy until the playoffs.

"Hard work's good for you."

"It'll pay off," I agree.

"How's the arm?"

"Good." I keep my answers short, even though I know what's coming. Every time Dad asks about my arm, a lecture about my pitching follows.

"You need to stay focused and take your time. Last week, you were rushing some of your pitches."

"I pitched a shutout against Central. That was damn good pitching."

"It could have been a no-hitter," he comments.

What the hell? How can he be on my case about my pitching last Thursday? It was the best game I've ever pitched. A no-hitter is a nice dream but virtually impossible against a team as good as Central. Arguing with him will make him angry, so I keep my mouth shut.

"Where's your phone?" Dad asks, remembering that I'm required to give it to him when I get home.

Guess we're done talking. It's not like I can say anything that will convince him I played a great game. He finds something wrong every time I'm on the mound. Choosing to stay silent is my best option. If he has more to say, he'll say it whether I respond or not.

Last night, he forgot about the phone, so I kept it with me until I was ready to sleep and then left it on the kitchen counter. Sighing heavily, I pull it out of my pocket and pass it to him. Dad accepts the phone, places it on the table next to him, and returns his attention to the game.

I finish my dinner and retreat to my room for the night. I have some homework that needs to be done, but I don't bother with it. I'm tired and sore, and my shoulder is killing me. It needs to be iced, but I'm too exhausted to go back downstairs and risk having to talk to Dad again. Instead, I take another shower. The water at the school isn't hot. Hell, it's barely warm. I never feel like I get clean enough there. We all take showers as fast as possible so we can get home. I don't take another one after every practice, but my muscles are screaming tonight.

The water is as hot as I can stand it when I step inside. I step under the rain shower head and let the hot water relax my stiff muscles. Then I take the massage shower head that can stay in place or be held and hold it close to my traps, allowing the massage head to work out my muscles. Moving the massager down, I let it work out my leg muscles, too. This was the best purchase my parents made when they remodeled my bathroom a few years ago. They knew having both shower heads would come in handy with me playing baseball year-round.

I feel better once I'm back in my room—the shower helped. I'm not as sore, and I feel more relaxed. Too bad I don't have my phone. Getting lost in pointless reels and mindless scrolling is the break I need. It's after ten when I fall into bed. I need to study for my science test and read some in the English book assigned yesterday, but I'm too worn out to focus.

I attempt to read some of Romeo and Juliet, but it's so hard to understand. Reading has never been something I do for fun. To me, it's a boring waste of time. I'd rather be outside playing sports. Izzy loves to read and always tries to get me to do it, but it hasn't stuck. She laughs at me when I roll my eyes or act like reading will kill me. She even tries to read out loud to me when we hang out in the treehouse.

Instead of doing homework, I pull the covers over me and pull the second pillow against my body, the conversation with my dad playing in my head. Hard work doesn't bother me, but I wish I didn't get my ass in trouble every time I blow off some steam. Going to Bomb's parties is my way of letting loose and relaxing. Last week, I might have taken the drinking a little too far, but that's a rare occurrence. Now, I'm stuck in the house with my parents for six agonizing weeks.

chapter
twenty

Sleep eventually set in last night. When my mom woke me, I felt refreshed for the first time in weeks. I can't believe I didn't hear my alarm. Mom said it had been blaring for almost ten minutes when she shut it off and woke me herself.

"Thanks for the ahi salad. It was delicious," I tell her when I get to the kitchen.

"I'm glad you enjoyed it," she responds. "You must have slept well."

"Yeah. Apparently, like the dead. Thanks for waking me. Where's Dad?"

"He had to leave early for the marina. They have several early charters leaving, and one of the captains called in sick, so he's going to have to take that group out. Maria is going to watch the bait and tackle shop."

"That's good." Maria is Captain Stuart's wife. She helps out when they are short-handed.

"I made some blueberry muffins. They're on the table."

"Awesome! Thanks, Mom."

"You're welcome," she responds, handing me my phone.

She makes the best homemade blueberry muffins. I grab two, tell her goodbye, and head for school.

"Let me drive you, Eli," Mom offers.

"Thanks, but I'd rather walk today." It's not far, and the mornings are still cool without being cold. Walking gives me time to eat my muffins.

"Okay. I'll see you at the game. Have a good day. I love you."

"See ya. Love you, too."

It's not even eight by the time I get to school. There was no reason for me to be here early, but there was no reason to hang out at home any longer, either. Since it's early, I grab what I need from my locker and go to my homeroom to read a little of *Romeo and Juliet*. I've only read about half of the pages required for Monday, leaving me only four days to finish. I have a game tonight and one on Saturday. Plus, I have to take a large group out on a charter with Captain Mike on Sunday. Anytime Mike needs help, he asks me. It's good money, so I only turn him down when I have a game.

As I try to muddle through Act I, I feel like I'm being watched. When I look up, my English teacher is standing in the doorway. She smiles nervously and waves.

"Sorry, Eli, I didn't mean to stare," Miss O'Neil comments. "I was passing by on the way to my class-room and saw you sitting here. I'm surprised to see you this early. Usually, you come barreling down the hallway at the last second."

I shrug my shoulders. She's right. I don't make a habit of being early to school, but lately, I can't stand being in the house.

"How's it going with *Romeo and Juliet*?"

"Terrible," I admit.

"What seems to be the issue?" she asks, walking into the classroom.

"I don't understand anything I'm reading. Like, what are they even talking about?"

"The language can be difficult to understand, but don't put so much pressure on yourself. You probably understand more than you think. Close the book and tell me what has happened so far."

Reluctantly, I close the book and think for a minute. "Okay, so there are two families, and they hate each other. Then there was a fight between some of the guys in each family, and the prince got mad and threatened to banish them from Verona. Now, there's about to be a big party. That's as far as I got."

"You understand exactly what's happening in the play."

"Really? I do?" I ask in surprise.

"Keep reading. I think you'll like the story. Be ready to discuss the first scene in class today. I look forward to hearing your insights."

"Thanks."

I've never had a teacher tell me I'm right about much of anything. Better keep this conversation to myself. Izzy will never let me live it down if she thinks I'm enjoying Shakespeare.

As Miss O'Neil leaves, students slowly start arriving. Soon, Coach is standing in front of the room and the second bell is ringing. Too bad there wasn't more time to read. The praise from Miss O'Neil made me interested in reading more.

I zone out as Coach goes through the same boring routine as every other day of the year — roll, announcements, lecture about something that pissed him off, baseball talk. Same thing. Every. Single. Day. One would think he could at least vary the script a little. He drones on for the entire twenty minutes of homeroom until the bell finally saves me from death by boredom.

"Yo, E," Bomb calls from behind me as I walk to my first class. "Wait up."

"What's up?" I ask as he reaches me.

"You still grounded?"

"Yeah, for more than a month."

"Damn. Epic party Saturday night. You should have been there. I'm having another one this weekend. You gotta sneak out."

"Not happening," I tell him.

"Come on, man. Tina Cetti's gonna be there, and she's got the hots for you."

"She's got the hots for anyone in a baseball uniform."

"But she's been talking about you for a couple of weeks. Guess it's your turn," he says as he shrugs.

"Yeah, like I want to go where everyone else has already been. No thanks."

"You're missing out." Bomb winks before rushing off to his next class.

Missing out? Is he insane? Tina has hooked up with almost every guy on the team. It's gross and sad. I can get a girl on my own. I don't need sloppy seconds or tenths or twentieths. Who knows how many guys she's screwed? I'd rather spend time with Izzy anyway. Not that I'm allowed in the treehouse while I'm grounded, but it's easier to sneak up there than out to a party. If I get caught in the treehouse, I doubt I'll get in as much trouble as I would getting caught sneaking off to another party.

The first three classes pass relatively quickly, and by lunch time, I'm starving. The stench of bleach and grease hit me as I open the door. Why does the cafeteria always smell so disgusting? The two smells war with one another and roll my stomach. I can't sit in here today. Some days, it isn't too bad, but it's repulsive every time they fry anything. Today, we're having chicken fingers and fries, so it's especially horrendous. As soon as I grab a tray of food, I push against the crowd and find a spot in the courtyard between the two campus buildings. One holds most of the classrooms, the library, and the main office; the other houses the rest of the classrooms, the gym, administrative offices, and cafeteria. A large courtyard with benches and a few picnic tables separates the two. Thankfully, there aren't many people out here. I find a table to sit at so I can eat and read. All morning, my mind kept going back to *Romeo and Juliet*. I want to read more and see how it all plays out. It's not a big secret, everyone knows how it ends. But after my talk with Miss O'Neil this morning, I have this urge to read and be prepared for class. It's kind of cool but a little unsettling. The only reason I've ever done any schoolwork is to keep my grades up enough to play ball. This newfound interest in English class is freaking me out.

Completely engrossed in the play, the bell signaling the end of lunch startles me. My plate is piled with food. Shit. I can't believe I read during my entire lunch break. I shove a chicken finger in my mouth and chew it while I gather my stuff, then eat a bunch of fries on my way to dump my trash and return my tray. I grab the other four fingers from my plate before I dump the fries. I can eat them on the way to science. It probably would have been a better idea to study for this test at lunch. Too late now.

"Where were you?" Cap asks, arriving at the tray return window at the same time as me. The cafeteria smells worse now. Eating outside was the right decision.

"In the courtyard," I admit.

There are very distinct, unwritten rules about where to sit and who to talk to at any given time in high school. During lunch, the baseball team sits at the tables across the back wall of the cafeteria. No one else would dare sit there except a few select girls. It's a bunch of bullshit if you ask me.

"The courtyard? We don't sit there."

"I did," I bite out.

Without another word, I walk away. I don't need to listen to him give me crap about where I ate my lunch. I have no use for the juvenile lunchtime behavior of the baseball team. Those guys think they run the school and can get away with anything. Well, there's a lot of truth to that. As long as the team is winning, the town loves us and the school is willing to bend some rules, like when I was allowed to retake my history test at the beginning of the season. It's not right, but it's how things are done. We also get away with being stupid at lunch. There's a water or spitball fight almost every day. The only time we got reprimanded for anything was last year when two of the guys on the team started a food fight that ended up getting out of control. We all had to run laps after every practice for the next week, and we had to stay after school and clean the cafeteria.

At the time, I thought the food fight was hilarious and didn't hesitate to join in the fun. Now, it seems stupid. The perks of playing baseball are nice. This year, it all feels different, though. Being around my friends isn't fun anymore. I don't care about girls, even a sure thing like Tina Cetti.

chapter
twenty-one

E xiting the locker room after a tough win, I see my parents and Captain Mike waiting by my dad's truck. At the end of regulation play, we were tied 1-1. It took two more innings for us to win. Bomb hit a homerun during the second extra inning with two outs and no runners on base to secure our 2-1 victory. With a win like that, there isn't much celebrating. The team knows we didn't deserve it. It was more a game of who didn't suck quite as much as the other team. Everyone on both teams played like crap.

"Eli," Mom calls, waving me over. My parents probably thought I was going to ignore them. The thought did cross my mind, but I knew that wouldn't go over well.

Slowly, I meander to them, not paying attention to my teammates as they scatter for the night. There was no talk of grabbing burgers or going to Bomb's for a party. On nights like this, we all go home to wallow in self-pity.

"The team struggled tonight," Dad states the obvious.

"Yeah, it sucked."

"You guys need to pull it together before the Tampa tournament."

"It was one bad game, Dad—the only one we've had this year. I think we'll be fine in Tampa."

I'm not sure I believe my own words. He's right, we played like shit. If we play like that in Tampa, we won't make it past game two.

"Your pitching sure didn't help them," Dad comments.

"No one played well," I remind him.

"Let their parents worry about them. I'm only concerned with how *you* play. You allowed too many hits."

"No one scored on me," I argue.

"Doesn't matter. Coach took you out for a reason."

"Yeah, to rest my arm before the tournament."

"Listen, son, you need some more practice. Leave everything except your glove in the car then grab the bag of balls and my glove from the trunk."

"What? I just played a three-and-a-half-hour game. I'm hungry, and I have homework."

"Don't argue with me," Dad barks. "Get on the field and let's practice."

I look to Mom for help, but she stays silent.

"This is bullshit," I mumble, throwing my backpack and baseball bag in the trunk.

"Marcus, can I speak with you for a second?" Captain Mike asks as I search my bag for my glove.

After gathering the balls and gloves, I slam the trunk and walk back to my mom. Dad and Captain Mike are a few feet away talking, but I can't hear what they are saying.

"My arm needs to rest," I whisper to my mom.

"A few practice pitches will be good for you."

I don't bother telling my mom that my shoulder is bothering me. It's been hurting a lot the past few weeks, but I've kept it to myself. The last thing I need is for Coach to find out.

"Eli," Dad calls as he walks back over with Mike. "I had a long talk with Mike, and he's going to throw some balls with you while I take your mother home. He'll bring you home later."

What? That doesn't sound right. Dad letting Captain Mike work out with me isn't like him at all. Usually, Dad wants to be there to tell me what I'm doing wrong.

"Okay. That sounds good," I agree before he has a chance to change his mind. Mike picks up the bag of balls and starts walking toward the field.

"See you later, son," Dad says.

"Bye, honey," Mom says at the same time.

I wave and then follow Mike. The lights are still on, but the field and parking lot are empty. Sometimes I come out to the field at night when no one is around. It's a good place to think. I like the silence of an empty field. Mike drops the bag of baseballs next to the mound.

"Toss me a glove," he calls as he walks toward home plate. He catches the glove and puts it on. I put my glove on and pick up three balls, putting one in each pocket of my sweatpants. I get ready, focus on Mike, and throw my first ball. He catches it and tosses it back to me.

"Good. Throw this one a little harder."

"Are you sure?" I ask. I don't want to hurt Mike if I throw too hard.

"I can handle it," he assures me.

The next three pitches are harder. He catches the first two but misses the third. He picks up the balls and jogs out to the mound.

"You look good to me. How about a burger?"

"What? That's it?" I ask a little surprised.

"I told your dad that I would work with you on a few pitches then buy you a burger. I didn't specify how many balls you would throw. The way I see it, eating a burger will do you more good tonight than throwing more balls."

"Thanks, Captain Mike."

After tossing the bag of balls and gloves in the back of Mike's trunk, I climb into the cab and close the door. He's is waiting with the truck cranked and the air blasting. The cool air feels fantastic. The mid-March Florida heat is stifling even once the sun goes down. Grateful for the air conditioning, I turn the vents on my side, so they blow directly on me. It feels good to rest my head against the seat and close my eyes. Breathing in and out slowly several times relaxes my entire body. It's been a while since I felt a calmness wash over me. It's a nice change.

"Alrighty. Burgers sound good?"

"Sounds great," I respond without opening my eyes. As long as I don't have to go home.

"Okay, where to then?"

"Seriously, Mike? There's only place to get a burger on the island."

"LBJ it is!" he agrees.

We have plenty of places to get good seafood, but no one can make a burger like LBJ. I'm starting to doze off when I feel the truck stop, and Mike cuts the engine. That was a short drive. I could have used a little nap.

"You awake?"

"Barely."

"I can take you home if you're tired."

"No." Opening my eyes, I look at Mike. "I need some time away."

He nods his understanding, and we climb out of the truck. Mike puts his hand on my shoulder as we walk to the door.

"Your dad means well. Don't let him get to you."

"Not as easy as you make it sound," I grumble.

Mike opens the door, and the hostess greets us immediately. "Hi! Welcome to Local Burger Joint!" she says with way too much enthusiasm. "Table for two?"

"Yes," Mike replies.

She smiles at me and giggles a little. "Hi, Eli."

Sorry, not interested. "Hey." I smile back. She goes to our school. I think her name is Marissa, and she's either a junior or senior.

"How was the game?" she asks, placing menus on the table.

"Good. We won." There's no reason to add any details about how poorly we played.

"Awesome! Congratulations."

"Thanks."

"Your server will be right with you," she states before walking away.

I watch her go. She's got a nice body, but I don't need any complications. Being a baseball player, you never know if a girl wants to date you for the status, or because she actually likes you. That works fine when all you're interested in is a few fun nights. Right now, I'm not interested in a relationship or a one-nighter.

"What's your favorite burger on the menu?" Mike pulls my attention back to food.

"Um, well, I haven't had one I didn't like. I usually go for elk or bison because nowhere else in the area has those. I change my toppings depending on what sounds good at the time."

"Hmm, I've never had elk. I might try that tonight."

"It's really good. It has kind of a mild flavor, not gamey, which I expected. I like it better than venison.

"Hi. I'm Chase, and I'll be taking care of you tonight. Can I get you something to drink?"

"Water," I order.

"Same for me."

"Okay, I'll be right back with those."

While Chase gets our drinks, I read through all the topping choices. LBJ has about a hundred to choose

from. It's insane and almost impossible to make a decision. The only items on the LBJ menu are burgers and
fries, but they have enough options for both for just
about anyone's taste. They even have vegetarian and
vegan options. You can choose your own toppings or
one of their signature burgers.

When the waiter returns with our water, we're
both ready to order. Mike orders an elk burger with
blue cheese crumbles, tomato, lettuce, spicy mustard,
and a side of Cajun fries. I order a Boardwalk Elk
with a side of sweet and spicy sweet potato fries. The
burger is topped with brie cheese, caramelized onions,
avocado, fig jam, and heirloom tomatoes. The fries are
tossed in cinnamon and cayenne pepper then drizzled
with honey.

My stomach growls as Chase goes to put in our
order. Suddenly, I'm starving. Glancing at my phone, I
see that it's already nine-thirty. No wonder I'm
hungry. The last time I ate was at lunch over nine
hours ago.

"Are you excited about the tournament?" Mike
asks while we wait.

"Yeah. It will be good to get away for a weekend."

"Your parents want what's best for you." Mike is
trying to play the part of devil's advocate, but I don't
want to see my parent's side right now. I'm still pissed
at them for grounding me.

"Well, they have a funny way of showing it."

"Being hard on you isn't a bad thing. Life's tough
and will knock you on your ass."

"Sometimes, I just want their support."

"You're kidding me, right? Your parents support everything you do."

"My dad is on my case all the time. Nothing I do is right."

"Think about what you're saying, Eli. Can you honestly say the times you've gotten in trouble and grounded were for no reason? You didn't do anything wrong?"

Mike is right, but I don't respond. Chase arrives with our food during the awkward silence. Instead of responding to Mike, I pick at my fries and take a few bites of my burger. When we arrived, I felt better, but now, I'm on edge again. He's right about everything. My parents gave me the punishment I deserved. Getting suspended, coming home drunk, and starting fights haven't exactly been some of my best decisions. Being punished for those things doesn't bother me as much as the constant berating I get from my dad about baseball.

"Talk to me, Eli. What are you thinking?"

I drop my burger onto the plate and sigh heavily. "I know I've made some questionable choices recently and deserve the punishments I've been given. What really bothers me is the way my dad treats me about my pitching. I'm a damn good pitcher and don't think I should be reprimanded after every game."

"I agree, which is why I offered to work with you tonight. It's not my place to tell your dad how to parent, but I felt you needed a break."

"Thanks." Having Mike understand my side is

nice. It hasn't felt like anyone has been on my side lately.

The rest of the meal passes too quickly, and before I'm ready to face my parents, Mike is dropping me off in front of my house. Except for the light in the living room, the house is dark. It's late, so my mom has probably been in bed for over an hour. Even though it's late, and I need to rest up for the tournament, I'm not ready to go inside and face my dad.

I'm don't make a sound as I go inside and lock the front door. Risking a look into the living room, I find my dad asleep on the couch with an MLB spring training game playing in the background. I leave the TV on and silently walk up the steps to my room, carrying the bag of balls and gloves with me. Leaving them on the floor by the front door might make too much noise. Once I'm in my room, I lock my door and start the shower.

Maybe being relaxed for the first time in months will help me get a decent night's sleep for a change.

chapter
twenty-two

Two weeks. It hasn't been easy, but I've made it two weeks without going into the treehouse. I miss Izzy and our talks. There's no way I'm making it four more weeks. Sneaking up to the treehouse won't be easy, but I need to see her.

Practice took forever this afternoon, and all I could think about was getting home. I didn't even bother showering. Coach was all over us after our shitty game yesterday and made us work our asses off today. I couldn't get out of there fast enough.

I won't have any free time this weekend because we have a tournament in Tampa. The bus leaves straight from school tomorrow to make the two-and-a-half-hour drive. We'll get in a workout once we arrive, but not a real practice, which is why Coach felt the need to overwork us today. We'll grab some dinner before our ten o'clock curfew then get some sleep. During tournaments, Coach enforces the curfew and checks our rooms at ten to make sure we're all there.

It's not like we can go anywhere. After dinner, we aren't allowed to leave the hotel, so the only thing we can do is swim in the pool or hang out in each other's rooms. Boring.

Our first game is at nine Saturday morning. If we keep winning, we'll play five or six games throughout the weekend and won't be home until dinnertime on Sunday. If we lose, we could be done by Saturday afternoon. As much as I want us to win the tournament, I'd like to be home Saturday.

Sneaking around the far side of Izzy's house, I stick close to the line of trees. Now that it's dusk and darkness will be settling in soon, my parents shouldn't be able to see me, but I take every precaution just in case. Circling to the back of the oak, I peek around it to see if my parents are in the kitchen. The overhead fluorescent light gives me a great view of the kitchen and dining room. Mom is at the stove, facing away from the backyard, and dad isn't in the room. He's probably upstairs showering before dinner or relaxing with a beer in front of the television. As fast as possible, I scale the ramp on the backside of the treehouse and rush inside, crouching down, so I'm out of sight. The ramp isn't easy to climb, but at least it blocks me from the view of the kitchen window.

Izzy is sitting on the floor with her legs crossed, her back to me, leaning over the little table. I freeze in my spot and watch her work. She's drawing today. Painting is her favorite medium. She puts on old paint-stained clothes, blasts her music, and paints the most beautiful scenes imaginable. But sometimes, she enjoys sitting in silence and drawing. She finds peace there.

Today, her blonde hair is flowing free, and she's wearing an old blue t-shirt that was mine at one time. I outgrew it in seventh grade, but it fits her small frame perfectly. There is a picture of a large fish on the back, and the front has the Ashton Marina logo. I have several newer ones that fit me. Every shirt I own is fishing or baseball-related.

"Are you going to say something or sit there all creepy and weird," she muses without turning around.

"I'm gonna sit here like a stalker," I tease.

Her infectious laugh fills the space. It's a welcome sound. I crawl over to her side, being careful to stay under the view of the window. When I take a seat against the wall, facing her, I see colored pencils strewn all over the table and floor. Every shade imaginable surrounds her. I lean over to see what she's drawing, picking up some orange, pink, and purple pencils on my way and setting them in her pencil box. It's a picture of the sun bouncing off the water as it sets with a small dock in the foreground. It's the view from the dock behind our houses. The page is full of all shades of orange, pink, and yellow with a little purple, blue, green, and brown mixed in. A few clouds gather in the corners, and soft waves lap against the dock. It's a beautiful take on the scene from our treehouse window. The water behind our houses sits to the northeast, but when the sun sets over the Gulf in, the array of colors dance across the water before it falls behind the tree line. I can hear, smell, and feel that drawing. Izzy amazes me with her art.

"Wow, that looks great," I praise.

"Thanks. I thought we could use some more color on the walls.

"We can never have too much of your artwork," I agree.

Her artwork is on every wall and the ceiling. Several have been here for years, some are new, and periodically she changes others out.

"How was practice?"

"Rough, but we need the work."

"Are you going to be in trouble for coming to see me?"

"Only if I get caught." I smile with a wink. "It's been two weeks. I couldn't wait any longer to see you."

She rolls her eyes at me. "You are impatient. I don't want you to get in more trouble," she softly scolds.

"I won't. I promise. Please don't make me leave," I beg.

"Fine," she relents with a heavy sigh. "What do you want to do tonight?"

"I don't know." I shrug and run a hand through my short hair as nerves shoot through me. "Watch you draw."

"Something better than that," she teases.

"What could be better than watching you?"

"Everything," she laughs with another roll of her bright, blue eyes.

"Nothing," I disagree.

"You never give up."

"Never."

She doesn't keep arguing, knowing we'll go back and forth indefinitely if she keeps responding. I watch as her hand effortlessly glides across the page, putting the finishing touches on her sketch.

When she's done, she packs up the rest of the pencils and sketch pad in the small bin where she keeps them safe. Then Izzy opens a tiny box and takes out two thumbtacks. She pushes herself up and hangs the picture on the wall next to the window. Every night at dusk, I'll be able to see a similar view from that window—the inspiration I paid no attention to tonight as I snuck up here.

"My parents are going to be expecting me home soon, but I'll stay as long as I can."

"I told you not to sneak up here. Your dad is going to be livid." Izzy drops to the floor beside me and leans her head against my shoulder.

"Yeah, he'll add time to my sentence if I get caught, but it's worth it."

"I hope not. I miss you."

"I miss you, too." I choke a little on the last word, covering it with a laugh. Izzy doesn't comment. The quiet chuckle lets me know she noticed.

Telling her about Boden is on the tip of my tongue, but I chicken out. Being on lockdown since the dinner at Poseidon, I haven't had a chance to share the news. My parents refuse to talk to me about it. It might be for the best, not that I'll ever tell my parents, but I'm still on the fence. This is the first time I have ever kept anything from Izzy. We tell each other everything—big or small. Part of me wants to lay it out for her right now, but there's not time for a real conversation about it, and I don't want to leave her to worry about my news for the next few weeks. If I get caught tonight, chances are high that Dad won't let me out of his sight, except when I'm at school for the foreseeable future. I can't do that to Izzy. She'll be heartbroken, wondering if I'm going to leave. Not knowing is always the hardest part. That's why it makes me so angry that my parents won't talk to me about Boden. Either say yes or no. If it's a no, I can get angry, upset, or relieved, and then get over it. If it's a yes, I can take time to work through my own feelings and decide if it's truly what I want. Ugh! I'm so frustrated.

Izzy sits up and eyes me warily. She knows something is wrong, and she's trying to decide if she should ask me about it. We know each other too well.

"Are you ready to talk about it?" she questions.

"Talk about what?" I feign confusion.

"Whatever has you in knots. You look distraught."

"I'm fine."

"Lies," she argues.

"Not lies."

"We both know that 'fine' is what people say when nothing is fine, but they don't want to talk about what's wrong. You don't have to tell me what's on your mind, but don't lie to me," she counters.

Dropping my head, guilt weighing on me. I admit,

"I'm frustrated about something, but I'm not ready to talk about it."

"I'm here when you're ready." She pats my legs before returning to the spot beside me and snuggling up to my chest. I wrap an around her shoulders.

"Thanks." I hold her close for several minutes before letting out a heavy sigh. "I should go. If I don't get caught, I might try to come back out after my parents go to bed. Will you be here?"

"Yeah, I think I can come back out later. What time?"

"Ten-thirty. Dad usually heads upstairs around ten, so that gives him time to make sure I'm in my room."

———

I'm back in the treehouse two hours later, waiting for Izzy. My parents didn't even question me when I came inside. We talked about practice while I ate the food Mom left me.

Her house is dark, indicating everyone is tucked in for the night.

"Izzy will be here," I whisper to myself. "Unless she fell asleep." Izzy sleeps when she's tired. She doesn't care if it's seven o'clock on a Friday night. It's one of the many things I love about her. She doesn't conform to anyone's standards. Izzy is who she is, everyone else be damned.

I get comfortable on the floor. I'll give her a few minutes, but if she doesn't show up soon, I'll have to go back inside. No reason to risk getting caught over a night alone in the treehouse.

When I open my eyes, it's still dark. I'm in the fetal position on the treehouse floor, shivering. The temperature has dropped, and it's pouring outside. I didn't plan to fall asleep. If I had remembered to bring the blanket out tonight, I would pull it over me and stay out here all night. *No, you wouldn't, Eli. You have to be in the house before your parents wake up.*

By the time I race across the yard, I'm drenched. The house is the way I left it, dark with the back door unlocked. The clock on the oven reveals that it's after two. Before I sneak upstairs, I search the fridge for leftovers. There's spaghetti and meatballs left from dinner, but I don't want to risk using the microwave. It'll make too much noise. Screw it. I'll eat it cold. I head to my room with a plate piled high with cold spaghetti. Between bites, I start the shower and get undressed. I shovel another bite in my mouth before stepping under the hot spray. The water feels great and helps me warm up from getting so cold in the treehouse.

Once, I'm warmed up, I climb out of the shower, dry off, pull on a pair of pajama pants, and sit on the edge of the bed scarfing down the rest of the spaghetti. I leave the empty plate on my desk and crawl under the covers.

I get comfortable hugging the pillow close to my chest. Thoughts of Izzy fill my head, making it impossible to fall asleep. I miss everything about her when we're apart—her long, blonde hair, the coconut smell of her shampoo, her artistic side, her silly side with all the corny jokes she tells that make me laugh harder than I thought possible, her serious side that craves knowledge, and the side that doesn't care what anyone thinks. She loves to dance in the rain, read novels, paint, draw, tell silly jokes, get muddy crabbing in the shallows, fish, and relax on the beach. Izzy is the best girl I've ever known. She's my best friend, and I'm completely in love with her.

chapter
twenty-three

My early morning admission still sits heavy in my stomach. It's the first time I've admitted my love for Izzy. *Am I truly in love with her?* That complicates things—a lot. I don't have time to think about this right now. Forcing thoughts of Izzy away, I finish packing my bag for the weekend, grab my baseball equipment and backpack then rush downstairs for breakfast. Skipping the last three steps, I toss my stuff toward the front door. It crashes into the wall with a loud thump.

"Eli," Mom warns from the kitchen when she hears the clatter.

You'd think after fourteen years she'd be used to me jumping down the steps and throwing junk in the house. I've been doing it since I was two.

"Sorry," I respond, joining my parents at the table.

I pile my plate with bacon, sausage, grits, and raisin toast, skipping the eggs and hoping Mom doesn't make me eat any. She always makes a huge breakfast the morning before I leave for a tournament. Her cheese grits and homemade raisin bread are some of my favorite foods she makes. Who am I kidding? My mom is a fantastic cook, and everything she cooks is my favorite.

"How do you feel about the tournament?" Dad asks.

Too bad I couldn't avoid morning conversation with them. No matter how much I try, my anger with them won't subside. I'm angry about them grounding me, I'm angry that I have to work at the marina in my free time, I'm angry about everything that happened last season, and I'm angry they haven't talked to me about Boden. It's been three weeks. They're taking their sweet time. For all I know, they've already told Mr. Barnes no. I'm not convinced Boden is the best decision, but I should be involved in the conversation. Every time I bring it up, my parents say they're thinking about it. If they wait long enough, Boden will make the offer to someone else. Maybe that's their plan—wait until it's no longer an option.

I felt better Wednesday night after my conversation with Mike, but the anger returned as soon as I came home. Being in this house is slowly driving me mad.

"Good. The first game should be a breeze. The teams from the panhandle aren't that good. The second game is going to be difficult. Win or lose the first, we play a team from Miami in game two. All the South Florida teams are decent. After that, it's all up in the air, depending on who's been eliminated."

"Double elimination?" Dad asks.

"Yeah. I expect we'll get at least three games. Hopefully, five or six."

"Team is strong. You'll do well. Are you pitching game one?"

"No. Coach has Mitch on game one and Sam on game two. He's saving me for later in the tournament when our opponents get tougher. I'll be playing outfield in game one and first base in two."

"Good, good." Dad nods his head several times in the most 'dad' movement I've ever seen. *God, even his movements annoy me.* "The team will need your arm in those tougher games. Your mother and I are going to wait and drive down in the morning. It will be too late by the time I leave the marina tonight. We'll probably miss game one."

"That's alright. You don't have to make the drive. It's just a few games."

My parents come to most of my games. They rarely miss one. There are only three of us whose parents come to out-of-town tournaments. It's nice and all, but the guys give me shit about it.

"We'll be there," Mom insists.

There's no use trying to change their minds. I glance at my phone and see that it's already seven-thirty.

"Gotta go." I need time to drop my overnight bag and baseball equipment in the locker room before homeroom. I grab a piece of toast for the road. "Bye. See you tomorrow."

"Bye, sweetheart. Have a safe trip." Mom stands up and hugs me. "I love you."

"Love you, too, Mom."

"Let me give you a ride," Dad offers.

"No, thanks, I'll walk."

"Let your dad drive you. You have too much to carry."

"It'll be a good workout," I counter, moving toward the door and gathering my bags.

I'm out the door before my dad has a chance to get his keys. It probably hurt his feelings, but I'm not in the mood to ride the short mile to school with him. I don't know why it's a big deal this morning. I walk to school every day with most of this stuff. I only added a couple of changes of clothes. Dad probably has an ulterior motive, like lecturing me about my grades, or giving me last-minute baseball pointers. Sometimes he takes his past life as a little league coach too seriously. Trust me, high school baseball is a whole different world than little league. Dad is in way over his head, but that doesn't stop him from telling me how to play. Usually, I listen when he talks, agree, which satisfies him, and then do what Coach tells me. This season has been different. I have no desire to pacify him. He grates on every single one of my nerves when we have a conversation.

I'm almost at the stop sign at the end of our road when Dad pulls up next to me in the truck.

"Hop in." The look on his face tells me not to argue, so I toss my bags in the back and climb into the cab.

He doesn't speak as he slowly pulls up the corner and looks both ways several times. There isn't much traffic this early in the morning; only a few kids live in this northeast corner of the island, and most of them are much younger than me. The elementary school doesn't start for another hour. He pauses several more seconds. Why is he waiting? I rarely see more than a couple of cars on my way to school. Finally, he makes the left turn and heads toward the high school.

"Why were you up in the middle of the night?" he asks. I freeze. *Shit.* Does he know I was in the tree-house? *Stay calm. Don't tell him anything. Just answer the question he asked.*

"I was hungry." There that's the truth and doesn't give anything away.

"I heard the shower."

"I fell asleep before I showered, then woke up around two. I was hungry, so I grabbed some leftovers and took a shower." Confident, I relax against the seat. He can't call me out for lying. Everything I said was true.

"It's not like you to wake up in the middle of the night. Is everything okay? Are you nervous about the tournament?"

"I don't usually fall asleep early, so I guess that's why I woke up. I'm not nervous."

He knows something. This line of questioning is weird, but I can't figure out what he's up to this morning.

"Listen, I know the past few weeks have been tough, but there are consequences to your actions."

191

Why are we having this conversation again? "Your mother and I had a long talk about this tournament. I'm not convinced you will be able to handle being unsupervised in the hotel, but your mother trusts you. If it was up to me, your mother would be the one driving you to Tampa, and you would be staying in *our* hotel room—not with the team. Do not make me regret giving into your mother. Do not break your mother's trust again by doing something stupid like getting drunk."

"Dad! We never drink during tournaments. That night was a one-time thing. *Once.*"

"I don't want to see you throw away your baseball dreams over a few parties."

"That isn't going to happen. Why are you always on my case? At least wait until I screw up before you ride my ass about it."

"You already screwed up."

"Not this weekend. But you're convinced I'm going to. You've already decided I'm going to get in trouble at this tournament."

"That's not what I'm saying."

"Then what the hell are you saying?" I yell.

"Watch your mouth, Eli."

Dad pulls up in front of the school. I hesitate. More than anything, I want to jump out and rush into the building, but he'll be out of the truck laying into me before I can grab my stuff. I don't need a lecture, or worse, a yelling match in front of half the high school population.

"What do you want from me, Dad?" I practically

whisper. The confidence from earlier is gone. "I know I screwed up at that party, but I'm paying for it. I've done everything right for two weeks, but you still think I'm going to go to Tampa and cause problems."

I look out the window and blink back tears. He doesn't get to see me upset. He doesn't deserve to know how his distrust is affecting me. I refuse to give him the satisfaction.

"Getting drunk two weeks ago wasn't the first time you screwed up in the past year."

"Can we not do this before the tournament? I need to be in the right headspace, not focused on what a disappointment I am to you and Mom."

Not waiting for him to respond, hoping he doesn't follow, I jump out of the truck, grab my stuff, and bolt for the school. By the time I reach the locker room, my chest hurts, and it's getting hard to breathe. I toss my equipment and overnight bag in a locker, then walk outside. Instead of heading across the parking lot to the main building, I turn left and move toward the trees that surround the west side of the campus. Even outside, I can't get enough air. What is happening? My chest tightens more as I drop my backpack and rest against the first tree I come to.

I try taking in a full breath, but I can't. *Breathe slowly, Eli. In. Out.* Telling myself what to do doesn't help. I can't get enough air. What if I pass out? Tears sting at my eyes, and fear encompasses me. What is happening? Why can't I breathe? Why does my chest hurt so much? Maybe I'm having a heart attack. I try again. Slowly in, slowly out. Again. Each time I'm able to breathe a little deeper until finally, I can take a full breath in and release it. My hands are shaking as I wipe the tears away. That was really scary. Afraid that any sudden movements will cause whatever just happened to happen again, I stay seated against the tree and pull out my phone. I have fifteen minutes before homeroom. Okay, I can stay here for five and still be on time. After a quick online search, I decide that it was probably a panic attack and not some sort of heart failure. Nothing like that has ever happened. What is wrong with me?

At least I was able to get somewhere private without being seen. The last thing I need is for Coach to catch wind of this little episode and call my parents. They would insist on me staying home and resting. Although, Coach might bench me. Then I'd have to stay home no matter what my parents say. Benched players aren't allowed to travel. It doesn't matter. No one saw me.

chapter
twenty-four

T he tournament in Tampa turned out to be a great weekend. We had a decent winning streak, and I managed to stay away from my parents. Bunking with my teammates was a welcome reprieve from my six-week sentence. After the incident with Dad in the truck, I half expected my parents to show up Friday night and force me to room with them.

My parents left this morning for an anniversary celebration. They took the boat out into the Gulf for a weekend away and will be home by dinner on Sunday. Two parent-free weekends in a row are a welcome change. Surprisingly, they are trusting me to stay home alone. Maybe behaving at the tournament worked in my favor. I could easily sneak over to Bomb's for the weekend party, but it's imperative that I stay out of trouble. Anyway, I'd rather spend the time with Izzy.

After an excruciatingly long day at school followed by a three-hour practice, I'm glad to finally be home.

The refrigerator is stocked with enough food for a small army. My mom prepared meals for me, but there's no way I can eat this much food. Searching through the containers, I find spaghetti and meatballs, turkey and black bean chili, chicken and rice casserole, a huge salad, hamburgers, buffalo chicken dip, tequila lime wings, tuna salad, macaroni and cheese, and baked chicken. *Score! Thanks, Mom.*

I preheat the oven and place three pieces of chicken in one dish and a huge helping of mac and cheese in another. Leaving that in the oven to reheat, I run upstairs to shower. The late March weather is stifling, and I smell like ass. I could have showered at school, but I would have been sweaty again by the time I walked home.

When I get back to the kitchen, I pile the hot food on a plate and open the fridge, searching for a Gatorade or bottle of water, but the stack of beers on the bottom shelf catches my eye. Without thought, I grab one of Dad's beers, too. Surely, he won't miss one.

It isn't easy to balance the plate, water, and beer in one arm and navigate the rickety pegged ladder leading up to the treehouse. The sun has fallen behind the tree line, cloaking everything in darkness. I pause briefly so my eyes can adjust before emptying my hands and searching for the lantern. With the flip of a small switch, the room is bathed in light.

Izzy will see the light on and know I'm here waiting for her. I dig into my food while I wait. Being alone for the first time is interesting. The freedom to be able to do what I want feels great, but it's also strange not having my parents here to hover, even though the distance between us has grown over the past few months. It started a couple of years ago but has become vast since last spring.

My mom was big on us having dinner as a family for years, but since my sisters moved out, I think my parents prefer eating alone. If eating without me bothered them, my mom wouldn't be so willing to leave a plate in the oven every night. Sometimes, she does it even when she knows I'm home. The first few times she didn't call me for dinner hurt, but now I've gotten used to it.

It's after nine, and Izzy hasn't shown up. She must not be coming tonight. Leaving my empty plate and almost full beer on the table, I take the half-empty bottle of water and move to the wall. Resting against it, I flip off the battery-powered lamp.

I need Izzy. Her presence calms my edginess. Why didn't she show up tonight? I wanted to spend time with her. As I sit in the dark, my sense of hearing is heightened. Closing my eyes, I listen to the distant sound of a boat's horn, probably a late arrival at the marina. An owl hoots, and the waves lap against the dock as nocturnal animals scurry along the bank. The sounds of nature soothe me as my eyes grow heavy.

The sun peeks through the window, casting shadows on the walls as I blink myself awake. My muscles ache from lying on the floor. My right shoulder is killing me from sleeping on my side. It's been giving me a lot of trouble lately, so I try to sleep on my left side, but I was too tired last night to think about it. Anyway, I didn't plan to sleep up here. Other than being sore, it was a good choice. I haven't been sleeping much lately, and a full night's sleep probably did me some good.

"Morning, sleepyhead!" Izzy's voice sings from the other side of the treehouse. I turn over and see her standing in the doorway.

"Hey." I smile, rubbing my eyes in an effort to focus. "What time is it?"

"A little before ten."

"Wow, I slept almost twelve hours."

I push myself up and stretch, trying to fully wake up. It's possible I had too many hours of sleep.

"What are you doing today?" I ask as a thought occurs to me.

Dad gave me the day off at the marina. No work, no baseball. A full day all to myself. I haven't had one of those in months.

"Nothing much," she comments with a shrug.

"Wanna have a movie marathon? We can watch out here on my tablet or in the house on the TV. We'll call it 'Monster Madness' or 'Horror Mania.' A whole day of scary movies and junk food. My mom made wings and buffalo chicken dip. She also baked three batches of chocolate chip cookies, two dozen red velvet cupcakes, and two trays of brownies yesterday. She dropped most of it off at some charity bake sale, but she left some for me. There're jalapeño poppers and pizza rolls in the freezer and popcorn in the pantry. It'll be awesome!"

"Yum! That sounds like the perfect Saturday."

"Cool. Let's go heat up some food."

"Can we watch it at your house? Your television is huge."

"Sure," I agree.

She's right. My dad bought a seventy-five-inch television last year and installed surround sound. It feels like you're in a theater. She runs home to tell her mom she'll be at my house for the day while I get the food and drinks ready.

Once the snacks are in the oven, I scroll through my options until I find the horror movie app. There are thousands of options.

"What do you want to watch first?" I ask as she walks into the living room.

"I don't know." Izzy follows me into the kitchen so I can take out the array of snacks I heated. I pile the food on a huge tray.

"That looks yummy."

"I already have drinks in the living room," I tell Izzy, picking up the trays of snacks and sweets.

Izzy follows me back into the living room, and we settle on the couch with the lights off and blinds closed. It isn't completely dark, but it's the best I can do in the middle of the day.

"How about we start with *Scream*? The first one since it's the best. Then we can watch the first *Halloween* movie," I suggest.

"Yes! Then we can watch *A Nightmare on Elm Street* and *The Exorcist*," Izzy adds.

"And when it gets dark, we can watch *Poltergeist* and...."

"*The Shining*," we say at the same time.

This is exactly what I need. It's been a while since we had one of our movie marathons. We've never made it past four movies in a row, but we're starting early, so we should be able to squeeze in all six.

I press play and wrap my arms around Izzy, pulling her to me. We've both seen these movies over and over, but she still likes to be held close. My heart races every time she jumps. Why am I letting her scare me? The movie isn't even that scary.

Izzy hides her face in my chest, and I pull her closer. She feels good here—right where she belongs. Ever since I admitted my feelings to myself last week, I can't get her out of my head. I wish I could make her mine.

"Do your parents ever get on your nerves?" I ask Izzy while scrolling to find the next movie.

"Of course," she laughs. "That's their job."

"Why is it their job? Shouldn't they be supportive and understanding?"

"Just because they get on your nerves doesn't mean they're not supportive. Your parents love you and want the best for you."

"You sound like my mom," I snap.

"What's bothering you, Eli?"

"Nothing. Everything. I'm tired of them being on my case all the time. I feel like I'm nothing but a fuck up in their eyes. No matter how hard I work, it's never good enough."

"Oh, Eli. Your parents aren't disappointed in you. We all make mistakes, and it's their job to help guide you on the right path."

"I guess." I shrug and press play on the next movie, not wanting to talk about this anymore. I need someone to see my side.

Izzy takes the remote and presses pause. "Sometimes, I feel like I disappoint my parents, too," she admits.

"What?" I ask in shock. Izzy's perfect. "You never get in trouble."

"Yes, I do."

"When?"

"I'm a teenager, too, Eli. Just because I don't go out and party or get in fights at school doesn't mean I don't make mistakes."

"Name one thing you've done wrong," I prod.

"I never do the dishes the first time I'm asked. Dishes are gross, and I hate touching them. I get to them eventually, but only after I've been told several times."

"Dishes? Really?"

"And my other chores."

"You've got to do better than skipping some chores."

Izzy looks down at her hands and fiddles with the blanket covering her legs. "When I meet you in the treehouse at night, I have to sneak out. My parents don't let me go up there after dark. I got caught a few times. My parents were really upset because they don't think it's appropriate for me to be up there at night with a boy."

"What? But it's me. We've been alone hundreds of times."

She shrugs. "It's different now that we're in high school. See—I'm not perfect."

"You're perfect to me."

Izzy rolls her eyes as she hits play on the remote and snuggles back into me. I never pegged Izzy for the rebellious teen. I guess we all do things our parents don't agree with sometimes. Izzy's words play in my head. *'Your parents love you and want the best for you.'* My parents do love me, but lately, that's been hard for me to see.

chapter
twenty-five

My sisters arrived home last night after dinner for a weekend of dress shopping and wedding planning. There won't be much time for us to spend together, but I'm expected to be at the family dinner tonight. Skipping it isn't an option. At least I don't have to go dress shopping.

My parents gushed over Molly and Emma for the entire of the night. I hung around, listening to tales of their perfect lives, Molly's wedding, and Emma's new boyfriend. That was news to me. At Christmas, all Emma could talk about was getting a ring from Jared. He decided marriage wasn't in his near future and broke it off with her on Valentine's Day. That was a dick move. She spent the night in a bar alone and this new guy, Gene or George or Gus. I don't know. Something with a G. Anyway, he was the bartender, and they hit it off and have been dating for the past two months. Emma is bringing him to Molly's wedding. It sounds kind of serious.

When I couldn't stand watching my parents fall all over my sisters any longer, I pretended to be tired and went to my room. After midnight, the laughter finally died down, and everyone came upstairs for the night. It's the first time my mom has stayed up that late in years. Tired must not feel the same when your favorite children are home.

The regular season is coming to an end in a couple of weeks. Then we'll have playoffs and hopefully the championship game. We've only lost two games this season, and one of those was game five in the Tampa tournament we played in two weeks ago. The last four games of the season are the easiest on the schedule. It doesn't usually happen this way. Most years, we have tough games spread throughout the season, or the hardest ones are at the end. Easy games at the end of the season are much better as long as we don't get lax. We can't afford to be cocky and risk losing to a crappy team. That could hurt us going into the playoffs, and it won't look good for those of us trying to up our stats for scholarships or the draft.

This is the second Saturday this month without a game on the schedule. Surprisingly, Coach gave us the day off from practice. I woke a little after seven and couldn't go back to sleep, so I got up and went for a run. There's a sidewalk that runs from the north end of the island to the southern tip along the east side of the beach and boardwalk. It's a good place to run early in the morning before everything gets crowded and the heat of the spring sun is stifling. Before I know it, I've reached the fishing pier that's more than five miles from my house. This happens when I run alone and don't have a reason to pay attention to the time. I end up running six or eight miles without realizing it, then I have to run those same miles back home. It's not a big deal. I have the stamina to run fifteen miles or more.

A few fishermen are scattered along the pier, but it's far from crowded, so I run to the end and back, which adds close to another mile. Then I turn left off the pier and head home.

When I run a long distance, I tend to adjust my pace without making a conscious decision. I'll go hard initially, then slow to a jog for much of the run and sprint the last mile or so home.

My music keeps me company on the run as thoughts of Izzy, baseball, school, Boden, and my parents war for my attention. Music has never been a huge part of my life. I listen to it when I run, when friends have theirs playing, or with Izzy. Music is important to Izzy. It guides her, pulls her out of a funk, brings her joy, and makes her cry. She created my running playlist over two years ago, and it hasn't been updated since. The playlist is a mix of rap, metal, pop, and country. Izzy's music genre changes with her mood. I love that about her. Most of the songs blasting through my earbuds are songs I had never heard. Now, I know them all by heart.

School is becoming a nightmare. The only reason I trudge through it day after day is for baseball. I've fallen behind again in two classes and need to catch up this weekend. Out of my six classes, I'm managing to stay steady with five C's and one B. Math and history are on the verge of becoming D's if I don't make some changes. Those also happen to be the classes I'm behind in. It isn't going to matter what my parents decide about my school future if I get benched for bad grades, Boden will likely rescind their offer. I'm still not sure if Boden is the right choice, but I want it to be my decision, not my parent's and not the school's.

Baseball is the only thing keeping me sane these days. I barely speak to my friends. I haven't been to a party since the night I got so drunk. There have been a few opportunities for me to sneak out, but the desire isn't there. After I discovered the peacefulness of the courtyard, I quit eating lunch in the cafeteria. When the guys invite me to grab a pizza or hit up Barnacles after a game, I turn them down. At first, it didn't bother them, but now they get pissed and make rude comments. Why don't they just quit inviting me?

My parents are another story. We go through the motions of being a family, but we don't exactly talk about anything important. I find any excuse to be late, so I can eat dinner alone. The only time we spend together is the occasional breakfast, when I'm not running late for school. Even at the marina, I avoid my dad.

Captain Mike is eager for me to help, so I spend my time at work on the boats instead of in the office. I'd rather be on the water anyway.

Sprinting the last mile leaves me out of breath when I finally reach my house. Leaning over with my hands on my knees, I take a minute to get my breathing under control. Having a completely free day is a nice change.

After a quick shower, I grab some breakfast and leave to go fishing. My mom and sisters have already left for a champagne breakfast at some fancy restaurant on the mainland and for their day of shopping. Dad left to go on some errands before I got home from my run, making it easy for me to get out of the house before he ropes me into working.

Dinner is at seven tonight, so I'll need to be home early enough to take a shower again before we eat. That gives me ten hours to do whatever I want.

chapter
twenty-six

"Hey," Izzy calls from the dock. Her long hair is pulled into a ponytail, and she's wearing jean shorts and a pink tank top. My guess is there's a blue polka dot bikini underneath. It's her favorite bathing suit, and she wears it almost every time we go fishing or swimming. It's my favorite one, too.

"You made it!" I wasn't sure she would show up, but I was hopeful.

I jump onto the boat then offer Izzy a hand and help her step on. We stow our bags in the compartment on the stern, so they don't get wet. Taking off my shirt, I toss it in the box. Izzy does the same, revealing that bikini I like so much.

As we settle into the small motorboat for the ride to the bay near the south end of the island, my phone buzzes with a text.

Dad: Where are you?

He probably has a list of chores for me to do. Too bad. I need a break.

> Me: Fishing.

> Dad: You need to be at home today.
> Your sisters are here.

Is he kidding me? They'll be shopping all day. Why should I sit at home and wait for them to return? That's stupid.

> Me: I'll be home for dinner. No one needs my help with dresses.

Not waiting for a response, I toss my phone in my backpack, turn on the engine, and carefully back out of the slip. If Dad didn't want me to use the boat, he shouldn't have given it to me. I push the throttle forward as soon as I'm past the no wake zone. The wind feels great. It's no speed boat, but it can go pretty fast.

It's hard to talk over the motor and wind, so Izzy sits quietly as we make the thirty-minute trip to the bay. She leans back on her elbows and lifts her face toward the sun, soaking up the rays and letting the spray hit her. She loves being on the water as much as me.

There are a good twenty or so other boats out here already but maneuvering around them to my favorite place to drop the anchor is easy. This popular fishing spot is one of the best places in the area to catch sheepshead, so it's worth the crowd.

I lather on some more sunscreen before handing the bottle to Izzy. She rolls her eyes, accepting the bottle and doing the same. She tans easily and rarely wears sunscreen unless we're together, and that's only because I insist.

While she rubs on the lotion, I pull out two rods and bait the hooks. Then I hand one to Izzy, and we throw our lines out. Now we can sit back and wait for something to bite.

It doesn't take long to feel a pull on my line. As the line bobs down, I spring into action, pulling the rod and winding the reel. The fish pulls back, but I easily reel in the ten-pound speckled trout. I toss it in the cooler, rebait the hook, and throw my line back. A couple of minutes later, Izzy gets a bite on her hook. I watch her reel the guy in while still keeping an eye on my line. Unless it's a huge fish, she doesn't need my help. When she gets it in the net, I see that it's a small flounder, probably around five pounds. She throws her fish in our cooler and baits her hook. Repeat, repeat, repeat. Three hours in, I have three speckled trout, each around eight to ten pounds, a small black drum close to forty pounds, and a few flounder. Izzy caught two speckled trout, some flounder, and two sheepshead. The tide is changing, and I need to go get more ice to keep the fish fresh. Plus, I'm getting hungry.

"I need to head to the marina for ice and food," I tell Izzy.

"Okay."

After a quick trip to South Marina for ice, food,

bait, and a bathroom break, we return to our spot in the bay. Boats have come and gone throughout the morning. Now, there's closer to thirty in the bay, and the heat of the day is reaching the nineties. There's no top on my little boat, so I make sure to keep reapplying sunscreen. There's nothing worse than sunburn.

"How are your sisters?" Izzy asks.

"Good. You know how much my parents gush over them."

"I can understand. They don't get to see Molly and Emma very often."

"I guess." I shrug. My sisters might not come home much, but my mom talks to them both almost every day.

"Are you okay? You seem down."

I shrug again. There's no reason to tell Izzy how much I don't like having my sisters around. I love them and we get along fine, but my parents have been so disappointed in me lately that it makes me not want to hear how perfect their lives are going.

"Can we just fish?" I ask.

Izzy nods, knowing I'll talk to her when I'm ready. I appreciate that she never pushes.

It's almost two in the afternoon when another boat, similar to mine, approaches. As they get closer, I see it's some of the guys from the team. Bomb delicately pulls up beside me, and we both drop fenders, so we don't damage the boats. Then Cap tosses me a line, and I tie our boats together.

Cap and Petey hop onto my boat while Jonesy, Bomb, and Sam stay on theirs. I position myself

between them and Izzy in a protective stance. They won't do anything to her, hell, they probably won't even talk to her, but I feel this overwhelming need to protect her.

"Whatcha doin'?" Cap asks.

"Fishing," I clip. I'm not trying to be an ass, but I don't want to hang out with them today.

"Catch anything?" Cap continues either not noticing my mood or choosing to ignore it.

"Yeah, a couple of redfish, some black drum, a few speckled trout, flounder, and several sheepshead." The afternoon has proven to be better than the morning.

"Nice," Petey compliments.

"Want a beer?" Bomb offers, handing one to Petey and Cap, then holding one out for me.

"No, thanks."

I don't make a habit of drinking when I'm on the water, especially when I have to drive the boat. Izzy doesn't like it when I drink, so I avoid it in front of her. That's one reason she quit going to parties with me last year.

If I don't listen to anything else my dad tells me, I usually obey his rule of no drinking on the water. When I was five, our family was out on a charter fishing trip—my parents, sisters, uncle, aunt, and cousin. We had a great time fishing and spending the day together. It was the first charter trip my cousin and I were allowed to attend—she was only four. The adults were drinking, but we had a captain driving the boat, so it wasn't a big deal. At the time, I didn't know this, but my dad's brother had a few too many and was completely wasted. He tripped and hit his head before falling into the water. The captain jumped in after him while my dad called for help. He wanted to go in, too, but then we would have been looking for two men. They didn't find my uncle until the next day. My dad blames himself. My aunt blames herself. It was a freak accident, and no one is to blame.

The accident changed my dad's attitude about the water. Since then, he won't have any alcohol if he's on the water. That includes the marina, our dock, and the beach. *'Water and alcohol don't mix, son.'* I've heard those words hundreds of times since I became a teenager.

After my uncle died, my dad's relationship with my aunt and grandparents was strained for a long time. We didn't see much of them for the next six or so years. Things are better now, but it's hard to have a bond with your grandparents when they weren't part of your childhood. They live in Key West and don't come to Ashton Bay often. My aunt and cousin moved back to Pennsylvania—where my aunt is from—and we haven't seen them in a few years.

"Suit yourself." Bomb shakes his head, disappointed in me for not drinking with them. None of my friends know about my uncle. It isn't a story I've shared with any of my friends, except Izzy.

"Are you driving the boat?" I ask Bomb.

"Yeah."

"Then you shouldn't be drinking."

"Uh, yeah. Okay, Mom," he laughs.

"Come on, man. I'm serious."

"When did you become such a drag?" Jonesy asks with disgust.

"Just trying to keep my teammates alive."

"I think we can take care of ourselves," Sam snaps.

"Guys…" I start.

"Let's go, Cap, Petey," Bomb commands. Petey scrambles back onto Bomb's boat and Cap turns to me.

"Sorry," he mouths before boarding the other boat.

I could refuse to untie them, but someone else can easily lean over and do it, so instead of arguing with them, I undo the rope and toss it back onto their boat, then watch as Bomb races away.

"I hope nothing happens to them," I mumble.

"That's not safe," Izzy comments behind me.

"I know, but they aren't going to listen to me." I turn to face her. "I'm sorry they were so rude and didn't acknowledge you."

She shrugs like it doesn't matter. "Thank you for not accepting the beer."

"Never on the water or with you. I respect how you feel about drinking."

The rest of the afternoon drags by as thoughts of my friends vie for attention. Every time I try to focus on something else or have a conversation with Izzy, concern for their safety pushes its way to the front of my mind. It's probably something they do often. I haven't been out on the boat with the guys since we were old enough to legally drive them alone.

At four o'clock, we pull our rods in and secure everything for the ride back to the dock. Tomorrow,

I'll clean the boat and return it to my slip at the marina.

The ride back takes close to an hour since our dock is past the marina and around the island's north side. Once the boat is secure, I toss my backpack over my shoulder and lift the two coolers out of the boat. They each weigh more than a hundred pounds with all the ice and fish. Grateful for wheels, I push one and pull the other down the dock. Everything else can wait until tomorrow.

"Wanna hang out while I clean the fish?" I ask Izzy, absently rubbing my sore shoulder.

"I can stay for a few minutes."

Izzy sits in the rusted lawn chair next to the prep area and props her feet up on the cooler closest to her. She didn't bother putting her shirt back on, and I'm enjoying the view more than I should.

Turning my focus to the fish, I open the other cooler and get to work, taking one fish at a time, cutting it open and cleaning out all the insides. Then I wash it, package it in a plastic bag, and toss the bag back in the cooler before grabbing another fish.

Izzy watches me work my way through the cooler.

"Are you going to talk to me?" she eventually asks.

"About what?"

"Anything. You have definitely mastered the brooding teenager."

"I'm not brooding," I snap.

She stands up, places a comforting hand on my back, and drops her head to my shoulder.

"Please talk to me, Eli. I hate seeing you like this."

"I hate being like this," I admit, slamming both hands on the table. My head drops, and I sigh heavily. "The past year has been hell. It's not fair, and no one cares. They want me to forget and move on, but I can't. No amount of time will ever get images from that night out of my head. It plays over and over day after day."

"I don't think anyone expects you to forget. Nothing about that night was your fault. It was an accident."

"It *was* my fault," I bark. "I should have..." I choke on the words as my body shakes. I blink several times, trying to keep myself from crying, but it's useless. A few sobs escape. Izzy waits patiently while I calm down. "It shouldn't have happened."

"But it did. You need to forgive yourself and try to find peace."

"It's not that easy."

"I know. Cut yourself some slack."

I relax against the table while Izzy rubs my back. She's my only comfort these days. Without her, I couldn't go on.

After a few minutes, I pull myself together, smile at Izzy, and get back to work. She doesn't push me. She knows I'm done talking for now.

"I need to go," she tells me.

"I'm sorry."

"I'm not leaving because of our conversation. It's time for me to go. You know I don't want to leave you like this, but I have to get going."

"I know. It's okay."

I watch until Izzy is out of sight then I get back to work. For the next hour, I continue to clean and prepare the remaining fish. I'm about two-thirds of the way done at six-thirty when it's time for me to get ready for dinner.

Before going inside to shower, I make sure the unprepared fish have enough ice. Then I put the fish I've packed in the outdoor deep freezer.

"Hey, Mom. Dinner smells good," I comment, walking in the back door.

"Thanks. How was fishing?"

"Great! I've caught enough to last us a while. Part of it's already in the freezer. I'll finish the rest after dinner."

"That's nice, dear," she replies. Preoccupied with what she's cooking, I'm not even sure she heard what I said.

chapter
twenty-seven

When I get back downstairs, my family is standing around the kitchen, drinking wine and laughing. It's a charming scene, but one I don't belong in. Emma is talking about graduation and her new boyfriend.

"I think he might be the one," she squeals.

I roll my eyes. That happens a lot around my sisters—the squealing and the eye roll. I grab a glass and pour some wine into it, mainly to see if anyone will comment. I don't really like the taste of wine, but let's see what happens.

Emma continues to go on and on about her life and how she can't wait to get a job and be out in the real world.

"College students are so immature. I can't understand why they spend all their free time partying when there's a whole world of culture to experience. George takes me to the opera and the ballet and museums. He's mature, well-dressed, and treats me like a lady."

"And then goes home and finds a fun college coed to fuck." The words are out before I realize I said them aloud.

"Eli!" my father bellows.

"What?" I feign innocence.

"Apologize to your sister."

"It's fine, Dad. Eli doesn't understand anything about culture or being an adult."

"Well, at least I won't bore my date to death. He's having fun somewhere if it isn't with you." *Shut up, Eli.*

"We have a great time together," she assures me with a tinge of skepticism.

Ha! Got her. I love getting my sisters riled up.

"Tell Eli about the dress you found," Mom encourages Molly in an attempt to get me to stop hounding Emma.

"Why? So he can tell me I'm fat, or that my dress is ugly? No, thanks."

"Oh, I'm going to tell you that no matter what your dress looks like."

"Mom," Molly whines.

Oh, yeah, you're ready for marriage when Mommy has to step in to keep little brother from hurting your feelings.

"Eli," my parents warn at the same time.

This is going to be a long night. At least I have wine. *It's not so bad.* I think as I pour a second glass.

Dinner was an hour of listening to Emma and Molly drone on about boys, dresses, and wedding plans. It was the most boring hour of my life. Halfway through glass two, my mom noticed and took it from me. No one asked me about fishing, baseball, or school. Guess my life isn't important.

After dinner, I finish getting the day's catch in the freezer then climb up to the treehouse. Izzy rushed off after our heated conversation, and now I want to talk to her before I go to bed. It's late and her house is dark, so I'm sure that won't happen tonight.

This is a good night to stay up here—no chance of running into one of my sisters. Glad to have a pillow and blanket, I take off my shirt and get comfortable for the night.

"Eli. Eli," someone gently calls my name. I blink several times, letting my eyes adjust to the harsh sunlight. Izzy is sitting next to me. "Hey, sleepyhead," she laughs.

"Morning. When did you get here?"

"Just now."

"I'm glad you're here," I say, taking her hand and pulling her down next to me.

"Me, too. You looked so peaceful sleeping I didn't want to wake you."

"I'm glad you did."

"You seem happier this morning." she replies, climbing under the blanket with me. I wrap my arms around her and pull her close to my chest.

"Dinner was long and boring, but I do feel better."

"Did you finish packing all the fish?"

"Yes. It's all in the freezer for us."

"What was so bad about dinner?"

"Listening to Molly and Emma talk about their perfect lives and listening to my parents tell them what amazing daughters they are was a little more than I wanted to deal with."

"When is the wedding?" Izzy stays calm and tries to keep the focus off my negative comments.

"July sixteenth."

"Molly deserves to be excited. A wedding is one of the most important events in a girl's life."

"I guess." Izzy's right. I probably shouldn't be such a dick to my sisters. They deserve to be happy.

It feels good to have Izzy in my arms. We lie there in silence, not needing words to be comfortable in each other's presence. It's always been like this with us. We can be doing anything, or nothing at all, and be completely comfortable and relaxed together. No conversations are necessary. I start to doze off when I'm jolted awake by the screeching sound of Emma's voice.

"Eli! Eli! Are you in that silly treehouse?"

"Yeah," I call back to my sister.

"Breakfast is ready."

"Coming." I look at Izzy, dreading leaving her. "Sorry. I gotta go," I whisper, hopping up.

"Okay. See ya later," she yawns, snuggling under the blanket and closing her eyes.

chapter
twenty-eight

The humidity is high, making it feel much hotter than it is Saturday morning as I step out the front door to walk to school. The late morning and afternoon sun will be brutal during the game. Saturday games are the best. Playing during the week after a full day of school is exhausting. When we play out of town during the week, it's even worse because we have part of a school day, travel time, and a game. Today, our game is away, but we only have to drive about thirty minutes. Coach needs us to be at school by ten to catch the bus because we play at noon.

We only have two regular-season games after today and have already secured a spot in the playoffs. It's a good feeling but not a reason to slack off. The better our record, the better our playoff ranking. Today will be an easy win if we play like we usually do.

When I stroll into the school parking lot, the bus is

waiting, and the team is loading equipment. Coach wanted us all here early to help, but I was up late last night with Izzy, so I slept in this morning. I'm sure Coach will give me shit about being late.

"Eli," Coach calls right on cue. "Get your ass over here."

"'Sup, Coach?"

"You're late."

"No, I'm early," I debate, looking at my phone. "See." I turn it toward him. "Nine fifty-eight. Two minutes to spare."

"Bus leaves at ten. We needed help loading. You should have been here at nine-thirty."

"Is the bus loaded?"

"Yes."

"So, you didn't need my help?"

"That's not the point," he argues in frustration. "Get on the damn bus."

I toss my baseball bag in the luggage compartment under the bus and fall in step behind the other guys filing up the two tiny, black steps. Teammates greet me as I make my way to the back. I grab an empty seat and put my earbuds in, starting the playlist Izzy created. Hopefully, no one will sit with me. *Fuck*. The thought barely enters my mind before Spaz, a freshman who barely sees anything past the dugout, plops down next to me. His real name is Chaz, but he's kind of spastic. Bomb called him Spaz once during tryouts, and the name stuck. He can't hit the ball worth shit but can run like lightning. Once in a while, he gets a decent hit but usually gets to first by bunting the ball or getting walked. Once he's on base, if the next batter hits anything decent, Spaz will make it home. He's easily the fastest runner on our team, but running track is a better sport for him.

Spaz is alright. We give him a bunch of crap, but that happens every year with the freshmen. I dealt with it last year. Our school isn't big enough to have varsity and junior varsity teams, so we have one team with twenty-five players. There are only three freshmen, and the other two have been friends their whole life. Chances are they sat together, and none of the upperclassmen would let Spaz sit with them. He could have chosen one of the empty seats and left me alone, but no such luck.

Spaz looks relieved when I don't tell him to go away. Instead, I keep my earbuds in and turn toward the window. He can sit there, but he can't talk to me.

Hopefully, we'll get some good players in the next two years. Most of our players are juniors and seniors this year. If we don't get some decent guys, we're gonna suck after they graduate.

Something shakes me and I adjust my position. My body is shaken again. What the hell? I pull my earbud out and blink my eyes open.

"We're here," Spaz whispers. He looks terrified, like he thinks I'm going to hurt him or something.

"Um, oh, okay. I'll be right out."

I didn't mean to fall asleep. I hate taking short naps. My dad calls them power naps. He can sleep for fifteen or twenty minutes and be completely refreshed. When I do that, it takes forever to wake up and get moving again. Slowly, I make my way to the field after everyone else has disembarked. If I take enough time, the other guys will unload all the equipment, too.

Coach is pissed when I finally get to the field. He shakes his head and turns his back on me. Well, shit, that's not good.

"Hey, Spaz! Do you want to toss some balls?"

I need to warm up, and Spaz is sitting on the bench alone while the rest of the team stretches and does various warmups around the field.

"Uh, really?" he questions reluctantly, eyeing me like he's trying to figure out if this is a joke.

"Yeah, really." He visibly relaxes at my words.

"Okay, that'd be great!" Spaz jumps up and jogs out of the dugout. We find a spot in the infield to throw the ball back and forth. I go easy on him because I know he won't be able to catch anything close to one of my fastballs.

———

A couple of hours later, we're up three runs in the top of the fifth inning. I'm on the mound getting ready to strike this guy out. I throw the ball, and it's clearly a strike, but the umpire calls it a ball. I throw my hands up in frustration. The umps have made some crappy calls today. Screw this—I'm going to show this guy who's boss. I throw the ball as hard as I can, hitting him in the shoulder. It was a dick move, and Coach is going to lose his mind. The player is clearly in pain, but he ignores it, drops the bat, and walks to first. The ump and Coach walk to the mound before the next batter is up.

"What the hell was that?" Coach yells.

"What?" I shrug. "Not my fault he can't hit.

"Watch yourself," the umpire tells me. "Pull that shit again, and you're done."

"Done? It was a fair throw. That batter sucks," I argue while Coach stares daggers at me.

"Son, I'm tempted to bench you right now. Not another word and keep the pitches clean."

I roll my eyes but keep my mouth shut. It won't do me any good to argue with the umpire or Coach.

The next few pitches are good, and I strike the guy out. One more out, and we're up. First pitch, strike. Second pitch foul. Third pitch, strike. One more. *Deep breath. Focus.* Ball sails toward home and… *Fuck!* It hits the guy in the side of the face. Good thing he has on a helmet, but it still knocks him to the ground. His team rushes to him. Our team freezes. The umpire and Coach run out to the mound. I'm toast.

"What the hell, Eli?" Coach bellows.

"It was an accident. I swear! I didn't mean to hit him. He must have stepped into the pitch."

"He didn't move. You're done!" the umpire bellows.

"Done? You can't bench me! I didn't do anything wrong!" I yell at the umpire.

"Go to the dugout."

"No! It was an accident."

"Don't argue with the umpire," Coach growls, pulling me off the mound, by my jersey.

I pull out of Coach's grasp and rush back to the mound, where the umpire still stands.

"What the fuck is wrong with you? You've been making shitty calls all day," I bark in the umpire's face.

"You better control your player," the ump snaps at Coach. Jonesy and Bomb join us on the mound.

"Come on, man. It's not worth it," Bomb says, stepping between the umpire and me.

"It's a bad call," I argue.

"Doesn't matter. You're doing more damage," Jonesy growls.

My teammates pull me away from the mound. I don't fight them, they're both right. The ump has the power to get me benched during the playoffs if I'm deemed a threat to other teams.

"This is bullshit!" I yell as Bomb and Jonesy drag me toward the dugout.

"Stay here and shut the fuck up," Bomb commands before he returns to the field.

"Jonesy," I call before he leaves the dugout. "Is he okay?"

"He was up walking around and seemed to be doing okay. I think he left with his parents."

"I didn't mean to hit him."

"I know." Jonesy runs back onto the field.

Jonesy believes me. That makes me feel a little better, but I'm worried about the guy I hit. A few centimeters one way or the other could have been a serious injury.

"Mitch, you're up." Coach sends him in to pitch.

Great. We'll probably lose now. I throw my glove on the ground and fall onto the bench. They can play, but I don't have to cheer them on. I pull out my phone, put my earbuds in, and scroll to my playlist.

chapter
twenty-nine

As soon as the bus parks, I rush from the back, pushing past the other players trying to exit. Ignoring the grumbles of discontent from my teammates, I make it off the bus first, grab my bag from underneath and start the short walk home.

"Not so fast, Sterling," Coach calls from behind me.

Shit! I knew he wouldn't let me get away, but it was worth a shot. My shoulders drop as I slowly turn toward him. I stand in my spot, unwilling to respond or walk toward him. If Coach insists on lecturing me, he can walk his fat ass over here.

He waits until the bus empties and the rest of the team is unloading equipment. Then he meanders over to me.

"Don't *ever* pull crap like that in a game again. Do you understand me?"

"Sure, whatever."

"What is wrong with you?"

"It was a bad call." I offer the same argument I tried on the mound.

"Accident or not, you know the consequences for hitting another player with the ball. It's hard to believe a second hit in the same game is an accident."

"I don't give a shit if you believe me."

"Look, Eli, this attitude and lack of caring has to stop. It's becoming detrimental. The team needs you, but not if your presence will cause problems."

"Are you kicking me off the team?"

"No, but I will bench you if you become any more volatile. Hitting someone with a baseball, especially as fast as you throw, could be deadly."

His words hit me hard, and I stumble back a step, recovering quickly. Coach doesn't need to know his words affect me.

"No one got seriously injured," I rebound. "You're being a little dramatic."

"Clearly, you have something going on in your life that you need to deal with. If you need someone to talk to, I'm here."

"There's nothing wrong," I lie.

If he doesn't remember what happened last year, I'm not reminding him. He looks me right in the eyes, and his whole demeanor changes.

"Shit," he practically whispers. His gaze softens. "Eli, you can't keep blaming yourself for what happened. It's been almost a year. It was an accident. That's all. There is nothing you could have done differently to change the outcome."

"I could have been there," I bite out.

"I know you're hurting, but if you don't find a way to heal and get past the pain, you're going to keep bleeding on those trying to help you."

"I don't need some mental intervention from you. You're nothing but a coach," I spit the last word.

I knock Coach's shoulder as I pass him. I'm heading in the wrong direction, so I take a hard right and rush across the street. A horn blares as a car screeches to a halt inches before hitting me. I don't slow down, continuing across the street. The driver yells something at me, but I refuse to stop. I have to put as much distance between Coach and me as possible.

His words stung, so I was an asshole back to him. He means well, and I valued his advice and opinions in the past, but now, I prefer if everyone leaves me alone. I don't need anyone's help. I'm fine.

Instead of going home, I walk in the direction of the docks. After the game, I managed to avoid my parents, but Dad's disappointing eyes reached me in the dugout. I'm sure they're waiting at home to lecture me on my behavior. After being forced to listen to Coach, that's the last thing I need.

I stash my bag in the storage building behind the marina and jog down the boardwalk. My muscles ache from the innings I played, and the tension I'm holding doesn't help. Pushing through the pain, I run faster, weaving through the Saturday afternoon crowds.

What gives Coach the right to talk to me that way? He was out of line just like that damn umpire. He can't help me, no one can fix me. I need the adults in my life to stay off my back. The first batter I hit was on purpose. It was stupid, but I was pissed off. The second was an accident. No matter what everyone else believes, I didn't mean to hit the guy. Playing dirty can be dangerous. Unexpected tears sting my eyes. I wipe them away and push harder, running faster. I didn't mean to hit him, did I?

"Fuck!" I grunt.

Maybe on some unconscious level, I did it on purpose. Shit! Coach is right. He might have a concussion. I could have killed him.

My breath is heavy by the time I stop, and my side is killing me. The muscles in my legs are on fire. It was stupid to run this many miles after a game. I only played five innings, but it was enough to strain my muscles. Barnacles is less than a mile behind me, so I walk there and get a table outside. It's too hot to eat on the patio, but no one inside needs to be privy to my stench.

I order water and a basket of fried shrimp with fries. Carbs are a must after that run.

chapter
thirty

Yesterday didn't get any better. We lost what should have been an easy win. There were some bad calls, but truthfully, if I hadn't been such an ass, I could have helped us win. Even after my run and sitting at Barnacles for two hours, I couldn't get Coach's lecture out of my head. I am bleeding on everyone trying to help me, but there isn't anything they can do to make my life better. It's been almost a year. If I haven't healed by now, there's no hope.

When I finally made it home, my parents were livid. Not only did I stay out for hours after the game, but I ignored their calls and texts. My parents were already mad at me for the way I played. They lectured me on playing dirty, hurting other people, making bad choices, and a number of other things. I tried to tune most of it out. Surprisingly, they didn't ground me.

This morning, I woke up exhausted and sore. I could have used a few more hours of sleep, but I had to be up early to work at the marina. Captain Mike asked me to go out on a charter with him today. When I accepted, I didn't plan to be awake most of the night. I need the money, so I force myself out of bed.

"Eli, how's it going this A.M.?" Captain Mike calls as I make my way down the dock.

"It's good. What do you need?"

"Check the ice machine on the boat and make sure the coolers are clean and ready."

"On it."

An hour later, six men are walking down the dock toward us. It's a group of college friends in town for a bachelor party. I can guess what they did the past two nights. They look more than a little haggard and hungover. I know that feeling, and it's going to make for a miserable day on the water. Their problem, not mine, unless they start puking. Then it's my problem because I'll be the one cleaning it up.

Introductions are made as they load a huge cooler of beer onto the boat. Guess they aren't that hungover. Captain Mike goes over all the safety rules and regulations, then leaves us to relax while he drives the boat several miles into the Gulf. We have about two hours before we'll hit the spot where we're going to anchor for the day.

They're giving the guy getting married a bunch of shit about his wedding and pounding one beer after another. They offer me several throughout the trip. I'm not sure what Mike will say if he catches me drinking, but I accept a few anyway. I don't get wasted, but I have a decent buzz going by the time we stop.

Mike drops the anchor and then helps me finish

setting up all the rods around the deck. Each guy has his own area with a seat. Mike and I will be on deck to help reel in the bigger fish and pack their catch on ice. Too bad I can't fish when I'm at work. It's allowed, but there usually isn't time for me to man a rod.

"How many beers did you drink?" Mike whispers, pulling me aside after we have everyone set up.

"What?"

"Don't play that innocent crap with me."

"Um, okay... Like, three," I admit.

"Look, I don't care if you have a beer or two at the end of your shift, but you know how your dad feels about drinking on the water."

"Sorry. I won't drink anymore."

Mike nods, accepts my apology, and goes to check on our clients.

Mike's right—it's hypocritical of me to be drinking today after I gave my friends shit for doing it a couple of weeks ago. I know how my dad feels about drinking. I never do it when I'm driving the boat, but I shouldn't be doing it at all. If something happens to Mike, I'm next in charge and would have to get us back to shore safely. Instead of sticking to my own convictions, I let a group of twenty-somethings I don't know sway me. I'm still ticked off about the game yesterday, Coach's lecture, and having to listen to my parents. It was an all-around shitty day.

Usually, being on the water clears my head. Today, I'm wound up tight. The beer didn't help me calm down, so it wasn't worth the hassle.

I follow Mike to the stern to help check on the

guys. Mike is helping one of them reel in a fish. At the same time, two others get bites. One doesn't seem to be having any problems, but the other has something big. I rush over to help. Together, we reel in the fish. The black drum must weigh close to seventy pounds. That's not unusual in the Gulf.

"Nice catch," I praise.

"Thanks. What do we do now?"

"I'll get this guy on ice while you bait your hook and try again."

"Really? You don't need help?"

"Nope. This is my job."

"Alright. Cool. Thanks, kid."

It doesn't take long to pack the fish in ice and return to the deck. By then, there are three more fish waiting to be packed. Two are in the reserve bin, and Mike is taking care to prep the other one. They can't stay in the reserve bin long in this heat. There's no water or ice. It's just a holding tank to get them off the deck until we can ice them down.

As the day progresses, I start getting into a rhythm and feel pretty damn good. At four in the afternoon, we head back with a huge catch and four drunk guys. Their two sober friends don't seem happy. I don't blame them. One puked over the side before they were done fishing. Somehow, we made it back to the marina without anyone else getting sick.

Only one needs help off the boat and to their cars.

Mike and I help them get their catch loaded in two cars, then return to the boat to clean up and get Mike prepped for his morning charter.

"You okay?" Mike asks, coming up behind me as I unroll the hose.

"Yeah, all good," I lie.

"How 'bout the truth."

"I don't know what you're talking about."

"You haven't been yourself in weeks." *A year, but who's counting.* "And you were drinking on the job today. What the hell was that about?"

"It was three beers. Lay off," I snap.

The sound of the water spraying over the boat's deck drowns out Mike's response. Washing the boat is more interesting than listening to him lecture me. My dad takes care of that at home. I don't need this shit from Mike, too. He's supposed to be my friend.

"Stop," Mike yells, pulling the hose out of my hand and tossing it on the deck.

"I have work to do."

I shove Mike with my shoulder, and he stumbles back as I grab the hose and turn on the spray. He comes up behind me and takes the hose again. We tug it back and forth, drenching each other in the process. Mike eventually gets it from me and tosses it onto the dock out of reach. Without thinking, I step toward Mike and take a swing at him, but he catches my arm before I make contact, pulls me to him, and wraps me in a bear hug with my back against his chest.

"Don't ever swing on me again, boy," he growls in my ear. "I don't know what the hell is wrong with you lately but handling it with your fist is unacceptable. I have known you your entire life and will do anything to help you if you want to talk."

"Nothing's going on!" I yell, fighting to get out of his hold.

He tightens his grip. "Come on, E. Talk to me," he begs.

"No." I throw an elbow into his side, not hard enough to hurt, but enough to force him to loosen his grip, giving me a chance to wiggle away. "Leave me alone," I bark as I jump from the boat to the dock and jog in the direction of my house. He calls my name several times, but I ignore him and pick up my pace.

When I get home from the marina, my dad is waiting on the front porch. Shit, I hope Mike didn't call and filled him on everything—me drinking, yelling, and taking a swing at him. Reluctantly, I approach him.

"What's up?" I ask tentatively.

"Relaxing." He raises his beer. "And waiting to talk to you. Have a seat."

Crap. I'm in trouble *again*. Why can't I do something right for once?

"Let me grab your mom."

He gets up, opens the door, and calls, "Evie, dear. Eli's home." She says something that I can't hear and then appears on the porch a few seconds later with her glass of wine and a bottle of water for me.

"Thanks."

I accept the water as she settles on the porch swing

238

next to my dad. My nerves ramp up sitting in the chair facing them, waiting to find out what they know.

"We want to talk to you about Boden," Mom starts.

I'm shocked, to say the least. I'm not sure how to respond, or if I should even say anything at this point.

"Okay," is the only word I manage to get out.

"We've talked about it many times over the past few weeks. Taking into consideration your behavior and how you are handling things here, we think you need a change," Dad continues. Wait, what? Are they implying what I think they're implying? "We think it will be good for you to be away from home."

Or will it be good for you two if I'm away from home? You'll be much happier when I'm gone. *Stop, Eli. Listen to what they're saying.*

"Really?" I question.

"Really," Mom says with a smile. "This past year has been difficult for you, and a change of scenery will likely be exactly what you need."

"What do you think?" Dad asks, catching me off guard. He actually wants to hear my opinion. This never happens.

Now it's up to me, but I have one problem. They waited so long to come to this decision I'm not sure I want to go anymore. This is my home. My friends are here. Izzy's here. My life is here.

"Um, I don't know what I think. At first, I really wanted to go, but I've had so much time to think about it, I don't know what to do."

"You don't have to decide tonight. We know this is

a big decision. I spoke to Mr. Barnes yesterday and let him know we'd have a final decision soon. He said we have until Friday," Dad explains.

Okay, less than a week to make the most important decision of my life. Something I always thought I wanted is mine, but I don't know if I truly want it anymore.

"Can I think about it for a day or so, and then we can talk some more?"

"That's a smart idea," Mom praises. "Who's hungry? I made shrimp scampi with angel hair pasta."

"I'm starving. Do I have time to shower first?" I ask.

"Of course. We'll wait for you," Mom says.

Wow, my parents agreed to let me go to Boden *and* want to have dinner with me on the same night. I thought my butt was getting grounded again when I saw Dad on the porch, but this night is turning out to be pretty damn good.

chapter
thirty-one

Three innings into our last regular season game, I'm waiting in the outfield for something exciting to happen. The team we're playing hasn't made any great plays, but they've managed to score four runs on us. We look good and are up by two runs, but Sapsville is holding their own. They've definitely improved since we played them at the beginning of the season. The outfield isn't where I want to spend my last game before the playoffs, but Coach is right — I need to save my arm.

Sam gets focused and throws a curveball toward the batter. Sapsville's guy hits a grounder past Sam and toward Cap in left field. Cap grabs the ball and throws it to Jonesy at second. Jonesy catches it a few seconds too late. *Shit*. The next batter steps up. Sapsville has men on second and third. They could tie the game if this guy hits the way he did his last time at bat. A homer would put them up by one.

"Come on, Sam!" I yell.

He winds up and throws a fastball. Strike one.

"That's it," Cap calls.

Another pitch. Another strike. This is good. We need an out right now. Pitch three. He hits the ball, and it sails toward me. The setting sun is in my eyes, and I lose sight of the ball. I miss the catch but quickly pick up the ball. The guy on third has already scored, and the guy who was on second is passing third. My only option for an out is to get it to second before the batter is safe. I need a great throw since I'm all the way at the back of the field. My arm is strong enough. Putting as much power as I can behind it, I throw the ball to Jonesy. As soon as the ball leaves my hand, I feel something pop, and pain radiates through my shoulder, sending me to my knees. I don't know where the ball went or if it made it to Jonesy. I can't focus through the pain as nausea rips through me. This is bad. I grab my right shoulder with my left hand and try to rub out the pain. Touching it only makes it worse.

Coach and Cap are both next to me when I open my eyes, and my parents are running onto the field.

"What happened?" Coach asks, kneeling beside me.

"It's bad. Something popped." I blink back tears as I try to explain. Fuck, it hurts. I don't think I've ever been in this much pain.

"Help me get him up," Coach tells Cap. Jonesy and Bomb make it to me right before my parents. Coach and Cap flank me. Coach has an arm around my waist, trying not to bump my injured shoulder, and my left arm is draped over Cap's shoulder as they help me stand. I sway, feeling a little lightheaded.

"Are you okay?" Mom asks.

"No. I need to sit down."

"Let's get him to the car," Dad suggests.

Cap moves out of the way, and Dad takes his place. Dad wraps an arm around me to keep me steady, and Mom walks on the other side of me. Risking a look at my teammates, I see the concern on all their faces. They lost their best pitcher less than a week before the playoffs start. Tears sting my eyes again. I don't know what's wrong with my shoulder, but there's a chance this could end my baseball dreams.

―

After several hours at the hospital, x-rays, and an MRI, we are finally heading home. I have a dislocated shoulder caused by an untreated labral tear. The tear is what's been causing the shoulder pain I chose to ignore for the past few weeks. The doctor said I shouldn't need surgery as long as I listen and follow his instructions. He relocated it while we were at the hospital tonight, which helped alleviate some of the pain. I'll have to wear a sling for at least a week, I won't be playing in the playoffs, and I can't do any heavy lifting or play sports for at least six weeks. The tear will heal quicker than the dislocated shoulder, but it could take up to three months to heal completely, even doing exactly what I'm told.

I've barely spoken to my parents since we left the ball field. On the way to the hospital, I was in too much pain to talk. Since I got some relief, I've been too angry to talk to anyone. I've been ignoring texts and calls from my teammates for over an hour. They're all concerned about me, but I don't want to talk to anyone.

Why did I ignore that pain for so long? This could have been prevented, but I would have missed several weeks of games. That would have been better than the months of healing and physical therapy I'm facing.

When Dad pulls into the driveway, Mom hops out and goes to unlock the front door. Dad opens my door.

"Do you need some help?" he offers.

"No. I got it," I snap.

He steps aside while I maneuver myself out of the truck. It isn't easy with one arm, but I manage on my own. This entire day sucks. I was already on edge, and getting injured didn't help my mood. I push past my dad and make a beeline for the house.

"Are you hungry?" Mom asks as I reach the stairs.

"No. I just want to go to bed."

I rush upstairs and slam my bedroom door. After fighting with my baseball uniform for almost ten minutes, I decide to skip the shower and sleep in my underwear. Getting the clothes off was difficult enough; I'm not in the mood to fight to put a shirt on. Propping myself against the headboard with a few pillows, I scroll through some of the texts. Everyone is asking me how I'm doing and what happened. They want to know if I will be able to pitch in the playoffs.

No, I won't be playing in the playoffs.

No, I'm not okay.

Yes, I'm in pain.

I don't bother putting any of my thoughts into texts. I have two days to let Boden know my final decision. Before tonight, I thought I had decided, but now that I'm injured, I might not be able to play ball. It's too early to know if I will regain my full strength. The doctor seems to think with my age and health, I will be back on the field, pitching better than ever in a few months, but I have my doubts.

"Eli," my mom cracks the door open when I ignore her knocking. "I brought you some water and a pain pill."

"Thanks." I take the medicine, which will definitely help me sleep.

"I know you aren't hungry right now, but I brought you a sandwich in case you change your mind."

"Okay."

"Do you need anything?"

"No. I'm fine."

"You'll get through this, Eli," she kisses me on the head and leaves me to wallow in

self-pity. I need to talk to Izzy, but it's getting late, and there's no way I can climb the ladder tonight. I find a piece of paper and a pen on my desk. Then I take off the sling, so I can write.

Izzy,

Tonight sucked. I got hurt and can't play in the playoffs. I

knew something was wrong with my shoulder but ignored it.
Now I'm paying the price. How could I be so stupid? The
injury cut my season short and might have ended my career
before it started.
I'm not sure what to do about Boden. I want to go even though
it means we'll be apart. I know you would never hold me back.
I almost didn't accept the offer because I can't bear the thought
of being so far away from you. You would never let me get
away with choosing to stay for you, but you factor into my
decision whether you like it or not.
If my shoulder heals properly, Boden might be the best move
for my future. I dread the thought of having to say goodbye.
See you in the treehouse!
Eli

There, basically legible. Writing without moving my shoulder wasn't easy, but I managed. I put the sling back on and get comfortable in bed again.

───

I thought for sure the pain meds would help me sleep, but at one in the morning, I'm still wide awake, holding the letter I wrote Izzy almost two hours ago. Quietly, I pull on a pair of gym shorts, not bothering with a shirt, and sneak downstairs and out the back door.

Folding the paper into a plane proves to be impossible. I fold one side, then turn it over to make the fold on the other side. It isn't even, so I unfold it and try again. One side is still bigger than the other. That will never fly.

"Fuck!" I snap as I ball the letter up. I rip the sling off and toss it on the ground, then I get in position for a pitch. Focus on the window. It's dark, but I know the exact location of the treehouse window. *Breathe in. Breathe out. Throw.*

"Ow, shit!" I cry out.

I'm not positive the letter made it to the window, but I don't care. Sharp pain shoots through my shoulder, knocking the breath out of me. *Inhale. Exhale. Inhale. Exhale. Breath through the pain, Eli.* I gather my sling off the ground and put it back on. My parents will kill me if they find out I'm out here throwing paper balls. There has to be a better way to get a letter to Izzy, but I wasn't thinking straight.

chapter
thirty-two

My parents didn't make me go to school today. They said I can take today and tomorrow off to give my shoulder a few days' rest. School is going to be interesting with my right arm in a sling. If things go the way the doctor expects, I should have my sling off before final exams.

I've been sitting in the treehouse for an hour when Izzy pops her head in the door.

"Hey!"

"Hi."

She walks across the room and slides down the wall next to me. "How is your shoulder?"

"Hurts."

"Are you okay?" Concern laces her question. I shrug a response. "What's wrong?"

"Nothing."

"You can tell me," she encourages.

I smile and take her hand. "I'm fine."

"You're not fine. You haven't been fine in a year."

"I know, but you can't fix this. You can't decide for me."

"I can never decide for you, but I can always help you talk through anything that's bothering you."

"It's not that simple," I growl, bouncing a ball off the opposite wall, catching it left-handed and throwing it again. "I don't know what to do."

"Eli, please talk to me. Is this about Boden?"

"Of course, it's about Boden!" I shout in frustration. "I don't know what to do. I want to make the right choice, but I can't figure out what's right."

"You love baseball. Boden is a great opportunity."

"But if I go, I'll be leaving you. Then what happens?"

"Going away to school isn't going to change what we have. We've been friends most of our life. Nothing can change that. Nothing."

"Everything has already changed!" I cry, despair hitting me in the gut. "Nothing will ever be the same. I've been trying for a year and can't get past this." I scream, punching the wall with my left fist. "Why is this happening?" Her papers and pencils scatter everywhere as the table flies across the room, hitting the wall on the other side and breaking into several pieces. "Why can't I get over this? Why does it still hurt so damn bad?" I bawl, ripping the artwork from the wall. I throw, punch, and kick everything in my path. It isn't easy hunched over in the small space, but I manage to destroy everything I can get my hands on.

Arms wrap around me, but I fight them off. "Let

go of me." The harder I struggle, the tighter the grip becomes.

"Eli," my dad calls, not letting go.

"Leave me alone!" I wail louder. I fight against his grip, pushing the sling off in the process.

"Calm down."

"No!" I pull out of his grip and lose my balance. Dad catches me, pulling me into his arms and to the ground next to him. "Go away!"

"Who were you yelling at, son?" Dad asks as I slowly quiet down.

"Izzy. She told me to go to Boden. I can't leave her."

"Eli," my dad speaks cautiously. "Izzy's not here."

"Yes, she is. She right there," I cry, pointing to the empty spot where we were sitting. "Where did she go?" I move onto my knees and start looking around the room and out the window. "Izzy! Izzy, come back."

Dad pulls me into his arms again. "She gone, Eli. She's been gone for a year." My chest tightens and I gasp for air, but I can't breathe or process what he's saying.

"A year," I repeat through gasps. "A year today," I sob, falling against him.

Dad remains silent as another sob rips through me. She's really gone.

"She's not coming back." Tears stream down my face as exhaustion weighs me down. I lean on my father for support.

"No, son."

"No! You're wrong." I snap, pushing away from him again. "She's here, on these walls, in her artwork, where we carved our names in the wood. I can feel her. I can see her. I can talk to her. She comforts me. I can't go to Boden; I can't leave her. If I go, she'll be gone forever!"

"She'll always be in your heart."

"That's not good enough," I yell as sorrow overwhelms me and pain tears through my chest. "She needs me here where I can protect her and keep her safe."

"Eli…"

"No! Don't say it! I have to protect her."

"She's safe now."

"I can't let her go, Dad. It's my fault. I wasn't here to protect her that night. I let her down. I'm not doing that again."

"It wasn't your fault. It was an accident."

"But I should have been here. I told her not to come up here without me. If the game hadn't been postponed, I would have been here."

April 24th. One year ago. The worst day of my life. Izzy and I made a deal when we were ten and helped our dads build the treehouse, neither was allowed in the treehouse alone. We made the pact because, at ten, our parents didn't think it was safe for us to climb the tree by ourselves. At fifteen, we still honored their wishes and the pact we made the day we carved our names on the wall.

A big storm came through the day before and rained out our game, so it was postponed until the next day. Instead of meeting Izzy in the treehouse to finish the birdhouse she was making for her mom's birthday, I was on the field. She should have waited until I got home, but she didn't. My strong-willed best friend came up here alone. As she reached the top, she slipped and fell. The fall broke her neck. When I got home flashing blue and red lights filled the street. We heard the sirens and saw the police car, fire truck, and ambulance pass the field as the game ended, but I never imagined they were racing to my Izzy.

I tried to get to her. I pushed past my parents, but a police officer stopped me. He wouldn't let me near her. She needed me, and no one would let me through.

"Izzy needed my help," I wail.

"There's nothing you could have done."

"I could have saved her!" I shout.

"Son, she died instantly. You couldn't have saved her even if you had been there when it happened. It wasn't your fault."

"It *was* my fault! I should have been there. Her parents blame me."

"That's not why they moved."

"Her mom said, 'We can't stand to look at you anymore.' What else could she mean?"

"Is that what's been eating away at you?"

"They hate me."

"Oh, Eli. That's not why she said that to you. Mary had just lost her daughter—her only child. She was grieving, and her word choice was wrong, but she meant that you reminded them too much of Izzy. You and Izzy were meant to be together. You loved each other since you were four. We all knew you two would end up together. Continuing to live next door and see you and the treehouse day after day was breaking Mary and Bob more than they were already broken. They never blamed you. They loved you like a son."

"I loved them, too. It was hard when they left. It was like losing Izzy all over again. I was afraid I wouldn't feel her anymore after that, but I did. That's why I spend so much time up here. This is where her soul lives. If I go to Boden, she'll be gone forever."

"Izzy isn't in this treehouse. She's in your heart and memory. She's in the drawings and paintings you have hanging in your bedroom. She's in the picture of her you keep in your wallet. No matter where you go, Izzy will always be with you."

"Are you sure?" I ask reluctantly.

"Brad is still with me."

"Really?"

"I'll never forget my brother and all the memories we shared, no matter how many years pass. And you'll never forget Izzy."

"I hope you're right."

"Why didn't you tell me you were struggling."

"Why didn't you ask?"

"Touché. I should have known her death was still haunting you." I laugh out loud at his comment. "What's so funny?"

"I know she isn't here, but sometimes I see her so clearly... Like, if I reach out, I'll be able to touch her. I talk to Izzy, and I hear her voice. Maybe she is haunting me."

"I get that."

"You do?"

"Yeah, I saw my brother for a long time. Someone would look like him from behind, and I would call his name. On the dock, I would see him sitting in his favorite chair, fishing, or with his feet propped up on the boat. I would have full conversations with him in my head and hear his answers as clearly as if he was standing next to me. He wasn't really there, but I knew my brother well enough to know exactly how he would respond in any conversation. You and Izzy knew each other better than anyone else."

I mull that over for a few minutes. He's right. Izzy wasn't only my best friend—I was in love with her, as much as I could be at fifteen. I didn't know it then, but I know it now. This past year has been brutal. I've kept a lot of secrets from my family and friends. Izzy kept telling me I needed to talk to them, but I didn't listen. Instead, I got angrier and angrier. Rather than talking to someone who could help me, I got in fights, drank, let my grades drop, and almost lost my spot on the baseball team.

"I wish you had come to me sooner," Dad interrupts my thoughts. "It was blind of me to think you were being a pain in the ass for no reason. I should have seen how much you were still hurting and known you were crying out for help."

"I tried to talk to a couple of friends when school started back, but they said, 'Get over it. It's been four months.' I couldn't get past it, Dad. I couldn't let her go, and no one understood. So, I bottled it all up and kept it inside."

"Your friends didn't know her well. Until you experience the loss of someone that close to you, it's impossible to understand."

Izzy had met some of my friends through the years, but they didn't truly know her. They accepted her because she was my friend.

chapter
thirty-three

My dad and I had a long talk in the treehouse Thursday night. It was after midnight when we finally went inside and got some sleep. It never occurred to me that he would understand everything I've been feeling for the past year. He always seems so put together and relaxed. He said I was too young when Uncle Brad died to remember how tormented he was. He felt guilty and blamed himself for many years. He told me about going to grief counseling and suggested it might help me. They tried last year, but I pretended to be at peace with Izzy's death and refused to go. Who knows why my parents bought that lie.

Yesterday, I spent much of the day in bed resting. I haven't slept much since I got hurt, and my breakdown in the treehouse took a lot out of me. My parents gave me the space I wanted.

I made the decision to go to Boden and see how it plays out. I can always come home if things don't work. Boden is what I need right now. Mr. Barnes wasn't worried about my shoulder once my dad explained the prognosis.

I feel more refreshed this morning than I have in a long time. A feeling of peace settled over me after the breakdown. For the first time in a year, I feel like I can move on with my life. It will be a long road, and I still blame myself, but I think I can eventually accept Izzy's death or least learn how to live without her.

The smell of bacon and waffles pulls me out of my bed. Saturday morning breakfast right on cue.

"Morning," I greet my parents.

"Good morning," they respond in unison.

"How is your shoulder feeling?" Mom asks.

"A little better," I lie. No need to worry her more. She doesn't believe me, but she doesn't question me further.

"Have a seat. I'll get you a glass of milk." Mom fills a glass and places it on the table in front of me while I pile my plate high with blueberry waffles and bacon. The waffles are delicious. Mom makes a bunch of different kinds of waffles, but blueberry is my favorite, followed closely by apple cinnamon.

Mom places a stack of letters on the table. During our talk, I told my dad about the notes Izzy and I wrote to each other, and revealed that I've been writing to her this past year. I offered to let him and Mom read some of them to help them better understand what I've been going through since last April. It wasn't an easy decision to allow them to read my most private thoughts, but they needed to know. I need help, and this is the first step.

"Here are your letters. Thank you for trusting us with them." Mom sits next to me and takes my hand in hers. "I love you so much, Eli. I'm sorry we didn't realize how much you were hurting."

"It's not your fault. I didn't make it easy. I hid a lot from both of you."

"Still, we should have been more in tune with what you were going through."

"I'm sorry for everything I put you both through."

"I think we can all move past that," Mom says, squeezing my hand.

"If it's okay, I'm going to go for a walk," I tell them, placing my empty plate in the sink. Usually, I run on Saturday mornings, but that isn't an option with my injury.

"Of course it's fine with us," Dad tells me.

"Thanks," I reply. Turning to my mom, I give her a hug. "Thanks for breakfast."

chapter
thirty-four

Thirty minutes later, I'm standing on the edge of the bridge that leads to the mainland. There's a walking path separated from traffic by a concrete wall. It's a quick walk to shops and restaurants in New Harbor, the small town directly across the river from Ashton Bay. There's also a ferry that runs every day to take you to and from the shopping district.

I climb onto the large half-wall that keeps walkers safely on the bridge, leaning against one of the steel beams, hanging a leg on either side of the wall. My heart races as I look down. It's a long fall onto a bed of huge rocks at the water's edge. No one would survive a fall like that.

The ferry passes below, making small waves that hit against the rocks keeping the water from eroding the shoreline. Everything is different now. Getting injured was always something I knew could happen, but I never thought it would happen to me. It was a stupid thought, and I knew I was playing with fire when I kept ignoring the pain. Convincing myself that it was tendonitis and a little ice and rest would make it better was easy, especially when I didn't pitch for several days. My parents didn't get mad when the doctor told them the tear had likely been there for months and couldn't heal because I kept aggravating the injury.

Having a complete breakdown in front of my dad ended up being the best thing that could have happened. I told him everything I've been feeling for the past year and how Izzy's death truly affected me. It was difficult to let my parents to read my letters, but it was easier than saying it out loud.

I'm disappointed in myself for the way I've behaved this past year and how I treated my friends, teammates, and family. Looking at the choices I've made through unclouded eyes has been tough these past two days, but it was good having a couple of days off from school. More than just my shoulder needed to rest.

Sitting alone in the treehouse, walking down the boardwalk, relaxing on the dock, and sitting here today, I've taken hours to reevaluate my life, to take a hard look at who I am, and who I want to be. When I lost Izzy, I thought my entire world was gone forever. Nothing mattered anymore, and honestly, I didn't care what happened to me. I make fun of my sisters and say I never want to get married, but that isn't the truth. I'm too young to know for sure what I want out of life, but I do know that I want to be loved, and that starts with caring about myself for a change.

My friends and teammates don't have much use for me off the field. I can't blame them. I spent the better part of a year pushing them away and not acting like a friend. We don't hang out much anymore, and I haven't been to a party since the one in February when I had to be carried home. I know I'm the one who pulled away from them and started fights, causing those friendships to collapse. I hope to salvage some of them before leaving for Boden in August.

My dad made a lot of sense when he said Izzy's spirit will always live in my heart. I'm the only one who controls whether I keep those memories alive or not, and I can do that from anywhere. The treehouse isn't where Izzy's memory lives — that realization helped me make the decision to go to Boden. It will be a fresh start with a new team and new friends. It will be a place where I can start over without living under the microscope of a town that knows my entire family, my entire past.

Someone walks up behind me. I hear the footsteps but don't bother looking. Whoever is there is probably heading to New Harbor for a day of shopping or work. A throat clears, gaining my attention. I don't turn my head, so the person walks around and faces me.

"Um, hey, Eli. Whatcha doin' up here?" Jonesy asks cautiously.

"Nothing." I shrug, not giving him a real answer.

He takes a tentative step up to the half wall and peers over the side. His hands are shaking. Jonesy doesn't like heights or bridges. I'm shocked he's up here. As far as I know, he's never walked over this bridge. Whenever one of us suggests walking to New Harbor, Jonesy makes up an excuse not to go with us. He takes a step back and eyes me wearily.

"It's a long way down," he confirms.

"Yeah."

"Why don't you climb onto the bridge," he suggests, eyeing the ground next to him.

"Nah, I'm good up here." Now I'm just messing with him. It's funny, but he's about to lose his mind. "I'm not going to jump."

"Oh, yeah, I know."

"Liar," I tease. He doesn't look convinced. "Seriously, Jonesy. I came here to think, not jump. Honest." I cross my heart like Izzy and I did when we were kids.

He relaxes a little but doesn't drop his guard completely. I don't blame him. If I knew one of my friends had been going through hell and I found him sitting up here, I would think the same thing and try to help.

I swing my right leg over the wall and hop down to stand next to Jonesy. Relief visibly washes over him.

"Better?" I question.

"Yeah," he exhales the word.

I motion for Jonesy to follow me. He needs to get off this bridge before he has a heart attack. Poor kid is terrified.

"I'm sorry," we say at the same time as we reach the end of the walkway. I lead us down to the rocks and find one big enough to use as a seat.

"What are you sorry for?" He didn't do anything wrong.

"For not being a better friend. You were hurting, and I distanced myself from you. It was easier than dealing with you, with what happened."

"You don't owe me anything. *I* was an asshole. You didn't deserve to be treated the way I treated you— none of you did. I'm really sorry."

Now that I've made a decision about next year, I need to tell my teammates. My dad and I talked to Coach yesterday, but I asked him not to tell the team yet. I want to tell some of them myself. Here's my chance to tell Jonesy, but I can't find the words. The past few days have changed my attitude about a lot of things, but this is harder than I thought it would be.

"I need to tell you something you aren't going to like."

"Is it about your arm? *Please* tell me you can still play ball."

That makes me laugh. Leave it to Jonesy to be worried about my arm and whether or not I'll get back on the field.

"I don't know for sure, yet, but the doctor thinks I will be back to normal in a few months."

Jonesy visibly relaxes, which makes what I need to say even harder. He's the one person I would take with me to Boden if I had a choice. After playing ball together for eight years, we are completely in sync on the field even when we aren't speaking.

My chest tightens, so I take a few calming breaths. After the big panic attack several weeks ago, I've had a few smaller ones. I haven't told anyone about them. It's one more thing for my parents to worry about, and they aren't hurting me. When I feel a little calmer, I look at Jonesy.

"I got offered a scholarship to play at Boden Academy next year... And I accepted it," I rush out before I can change my mind.

"What?" Jonesy tries to cover the shock, but it doesn't work. There's also a tinge of anger glinting in his eyes. "Boden? Are you *serious*?"

"Yeah. A recruiter came earlier in the season and offered me a spot as a starting pitcher, but I didn't decide to go until yesterday. We told Coach, but I wanted to tell you, Bomb, and Cap myself. He's going to tell the rest of the team next week."

"This is a big deal," he smiles as the words form. "This is a step to the majors. Boden graduates the best players in the league. Damn, boy, you're really going to go all the way!" He pats my good shoulder. "I'm happy for you. Congratulations!"

"Thanks. I thought you were going to be mad."

"Oh, I'm pissed that we're losing you—baseball won't be the same. But I'd be a pretty shitty friend if I wasn't excited for you. Can't I be sad for the team and happy for you at the same time?"

"Sure. Thanks for everything." Standing up, I brush the dirt off my shorts. "You drive out here?"

"Yeah. I was heading to New Harbor when I saw you on the bridge."

"Do you have somewhere to be?"

"No. I needed to get out of the house. I'm too pumped about the playoffs to sit still."

Jonesy gets like that anytime something big is happening. He has all this pent-up energy and has to release it. He's like a caged animal if he stays indoors too long.

"Let's grab a burger. I'll text Cap and Bomb. We have a lot to talk about."

———

For the rest of the afternoon, the four of us talk over burgers and milkshakes at LBJ. I tell them about Boden and how it all happened. I talk about Izzy. I even tell them about my breakdown and the panic attacks. Cap talks about Lindsay and how their relationship is going. He sounds like he's falling hard. Bomb talks about college and his full ride to the University of Florida. He could have entered the draft but decided to go to college first. It's a smart move, and one I've put a little thought into recently. Jonesy talks about his summer job at the local baseball camp. He's going to be a great coach one day.

It's been a long time since I felt this good about anything. For the first time in months, I feel like these guys are my friends again. I'm going to be at every playoff game cheering my team on all the way to State.

Monday, I have my first appointment with the grief counselor. It's taken a year to start this process, but I'm finally ready to get on the right track. It isn't going to be an easy road, but I'll make it through.

Cap and Bomb reacted the same way as Jonesy to my Boden news. They are disappointed that I'm leaving the team, but excited about my new opportunity. We have some good pitchers, but I was too arrogant to admit that. Mitch is stepping in as the number one pitcher next year. He'll do good things for our team. The team is more than just its pitchers, and we have some of the best outfielders, basemen, and hitters in the state. The Ashton Anglers will be fine without me.

epilogue

My parents left me at Boden nine days ago, and classes started a week later. New students have to move in five days before everyone else to get acclimated to the campus and go through orientation. My roommate has been at Boden since his freshman year and seems pretty nice. He plays first base and, from what I hear, is a damn good player. Then again, all the athletes at Boden are top-notch.

Today is my seventeenth birthday. Everything feels off about this birthday. It's the first one I've spent away from my family. We didn't have the end of summer party this year because I was preparing to move, and I'm away from my friends.

The summer was better than the spring. The counselor I've been seeing helped me learn how to start dealing with Izzy's death. I'm going to continue seeing her via telehealth until I can find a counselor close to Boden. It will be a long time before I can do this on my own. Getting the help I need was the best decision I made in a long time—other than Boden.

It hasn't been easy bearing my soul to someone, but it's getting better, and my relationships with my parents and friends have improved. Even though it was hard to leave everyone behind, I'm glad I chose Boden. This change will be good for me—I need a fresh start.

"Eli, you ready?" Devon, my roommate, calls from the doorway.

"Meet you downstairs in five," I tell him. My new friends got us off-campus passes for a few hours so we can go out to dinner for my birthday.

Falling onto my bed, I stare at the picture of the treehouse Izzy drew for me on my twelfth birthday. Then I pull the envelope out from under my pillow. When Izzy turned thirteen a month before me, she sat down and wrote me seven letters, one for each of my teen birthdays. She made me promise not to open any of them early. I was tempted to read the remaining four after she died but forced myself to wait. 'Eli-17' is written in large bubble letters on the front of the red envelope. Izzy loved anything with color. She always said she didn't have a favorite because all colors are beautiful.

My hands shake as I open the letter. I've been waiting all day for a few minutes alone to read this.

Hi, Eli!

Happy Seventeenth Birthday!! I hope your school year is great this year. We will be halfway through high school and planning for our next chapter by the time you open this. Maybe we'll even go to the same college on athletic scholarships. You can play baseball, and I can play soccer. When we aren't on the field, we can study together. We will have the best time!

Thank you for being by my side and being my best friend. I love that you are always there for me no matter what. I love you, Eli. You're the most genuine, loyal, funny, and supportive person I know.

Know that I'm proud of you. I'm sure by now, you're the star Ashton Anglers' pitcher. I hope your seventeenth year is everything you want it to be. You deserve the very best.

I can't wait to discover what memories we'll make this year on your birthday. It will be epic!

Love you,
Izzy 🤍

Tears sting my eyes as I fold the letter and put it back in its envelope. Then I climb off the bed and carefully place it in the metal cash box with all her other letters. Izzy was full of insight and wiser than her years. She was the best person I've ever known, and I miss her like crazy.

Anytime I miss her, I reread her letters and it feels like she's with me. I can hear her voice in the words she wrote. It soothes the ache in my heart when I miss her the most. Days like today are difficult, but seventeen was a little easier than sixteen — the first birthday without her. We had big plans to celebrate our sixteenth birthday together. As Izzy always said, *'It was going to be epic!'* I lost her before our birthdays. It was far from epic. I trudged through the summer party that was supposed to be our biggest celebration. It was a day I didn't think I would get through, but somehow, I made it.

This year has been easier. I'm getting the help I need, I'm in a better place, and I'm happy. I'll never stop missing Izzy, but deep down in my soul, I know now that I can survive without her.

acknowledgments

I would like to thank the following people for their support as I worked to complete Soul of Eli. This journey started several years ago when I left my twenty-year career to pursue my dream. The first edition of Soul of Eli was released in 2022. I'm excited for this second edition with a new cover and updated edits.

First and foremost, to my amazing readers. Without your support, I wouldn't be able to what I love. You have made my lifelong dream a reality.

Rick, my husband, for his constant support and love. I am grateful for everything you have done for me over the years. You are a true partner. I appreciate you sharing my excitement, helping me work through scenes and answering questions.

My sons, Anders and Grady, for your love and understanding. It has been an amazing Adventureland I am blessed to have you. Thank you for always standing by my side.

My beta readers, Danielle, Kim M., Patty, and Wendy for your feedback and advice.

My friend, Christine, for answering all my high school baseball questions.

My cover artist for a beautiful cover than perfectly fits my vision.

My proofreader, Michele. Thank you for catching my mistakes at the last minute.

My editor, Brittany, at Brittany Montano Management for editing the book and helping with the relaunch. I appreciate your unwavering support.

about the author

Pamela Gail was born and raised in southeast Georgia. She is married and has two sons. Pamela has always found peace and solitude in reading and writing. She expresses herself through stories that relay her deep appreciation of relationships and finding one's people, whether biological or chosen. Her hobbies include writing, reading, listening to music, wine tasting, and watching football. She also writes under the pen name Emerson Gail.

Connect with Pamela Gail by visiting https://linktr.ee/authorpamelagail to find links to her other books, newsletter, website, social media, and more!

Connect with Emerson Gail by visiting https://linktr.ee/authoremersongail.com to find links to her other books, newsletter, website, social media, and more!

also by the author

Book by Pamela Gail

Where the Path Leads Series

Path of the Heartbeats

Fixing My Path

Changing My Path

The Empty Path

An Unexpected Path

The Wrong Path

MM Sports Romance

Miami Vices

Books By Emerson Gail

Finding Forever Series

Finding Home

Finding Support

Signed Paperbacks can also be ordered directly from the author at www.brackishpublishing.com.